THE FOURTH HORSEMAN

A murder in Sheriff Hall's county coincides with the appearance of a phantom rider. Like an omen, it is there at every shooting. People scoff, but Hall has faith in his theory, and is ready when another cowman is shot in the back. Just as people are beginning to trust him, a stranger rides into town, making quite an impression on the folks in Bannonville. He makes an impression on Hall too, but it is a very different one.

MARTIN BISHOP

◆

THE FOURTH HORSEMAN

Complete and Unabridged

LINFORD
Leicester

First published in Great Britain in 1989 by
Robert Hale Limited
London

First Linford Edition
published August 1991
by arrangement with
Robert Hale Limited, London

British Library CIP Data

Bishop, Martin
  The fourth horseman.—Large print ed.—
Linford western library
I. Title
823.914 [F]

ISBN 0–7089–7037–0

Published by
F. A. Thorpe (Publishing) Ltd.
Anstey, Leicestershire
Set by Words & Graphics Ltd.
Anstey, Leicestershire
Printed and bound in Great Britain by
T. J. Press (Padstow) Ltd., Padstow, Cornwall

1

A Phantom Rider

THE story had lost some credibility by the time it reached Sheriff Mark Hall of Fancher County. He listened to everything a pair of townsmen had to say, then rode six miles west to the yard of Benton Talbot's ranch, known by its brand, The Goblet, and called locally The Lard Bucket, found Talbot out back where dust hung above a round, pole corral where two riders were doing their profane utmost to get a gunny-sack blinder on the face of a big roan stud colt who knew more ways to duck his head than most horses ever figured out.

Benton Talbot was a big cowman, and he had the assured, unruffled way of moving and talking that went with success. He met Sheriff Hall out front of the barn in shade and offered his hospitality after a handshake. Benton Talbot had a little age on him but it only showed in his lined and weathered face and the colour of his shaggy mane.

He and Mark Hall had known one another for many years. They were roughly the same size and heft. Both were big-boned men. The most noticeable difference between them was that Sheriff Hall was easily twenty years younger than the cowman.

When Hall stepped into barn-shade to pull off his gloves he said, "There's a story going around town that your riders have seen a man on a black horse who seems to have nothing to do but ride around spying out the country."

Talbot settled both shoulders against the barn wall of grey logs at his back before replying. "Yeah. They've seen him and they're both drinkers."

Sheriff Hall turned. "You don't believe they've seen him?"

"Mark, they've seen him at a distance four times. I rode out there the last two times, rode all over hell and couldn't find any horse tracks. What would you think?"

Sheriff Hall went to work rolling a smoke. "Drinkers?"

"Yes."

"Why don't you fire them, Ben?"

"Well, for one thing, they're my best ropers and although I've never seen either one them drunk, and I got a rule about having liquor on the ranch, I know they drink. I've smelled it on their breath quite a few times right after breakfast."

The big cowman tipped down his hat and squinted eastward where he owned the range to within a mile of town. "I've known a lot of men who couldn't get untracked in the morning before they had something to oil their joints. My paw was like that." He turned slowly to regard his old friend. "All I can say is that I didn't find any sign of a horseman out yonder, and I looked pretty hard. I also know they're good riders, top hands, hard workers. Now, what would you do?"

The sheriff ruefully smiled. "The same as you're doing."

3

Talbot nodded as though that finished the topic, but it hadn't for the sheriff. "Mind if I ride around on your range, Ben?"

"Not at all. You don't have to ask," Talbot said, and grinned. "You never asked before. Mark, he don't exist. I don't know what they saw but it wasn't a man on a horse."

"Maybe not," stated the lawman. "But I've been at this law business a long time and that's about how horse thieves work. They do a lot of scouting first. The successful ones, and the other kind don't last long enough to worry about. You got a lot of horses out there."

Ben Talbot hoisted one scuffed boot to the wall at his back and went back to squinting eastward. In a slow, detailed tone he said, "Ben, the first time they claimed they saw him was early last spring. It's getting along toward autumn now and as far as I know we haven't lost a single horse or cow. So, if I believed he was out there, I'd have to say he's maybe some grubliner, maybe

4

someone who likes the country. Maybe even an outlaw who disappears when he sees other horsemen. But tell me how he gets around without leaving tracks, and if he's a thief why haven't I lost any livestock?"

Sheriff Hall remained silent so long the cowman straightened off the barn, slapped him on the shoulder and said, "Come on around back. We're trying to get a saddle on a stud colt that's too clever for his own good."

But the sheriff declined. As he was riding northward from the yard, Ben Talbot watched him go and wagged his head. He wasn't going to find anything. No tracks and no phantom rider.

It might have been wasted time, as Talbot clearly thought it was, but the two Lard Bucket riders were not the only ones who had seen the horseman. Both of the townsmen who told Hall about sighting the rider were not the first who claimed that distinction, but one was Bannonville's wheelwright and blacksmith, a man of few words, little imagination, and a forthright, direct and simple way of seeing his life and his world. If he hadn't been positive he'd seen the rider he'd have kept quiet.

The other man was corralyard foreman for The Pine Cone Stage and Drayage Company in town. He was another individual whom Sheriff Hall had known for years. He would be no more liable to hallucinations or wild imaginings than the town blacksmith, and he would have been just as reticent if he hadn't been certain of what he saw.

But riding Lard Bucket range turned up nothing for Sheriff Hall. He was not a man to whom a mystery was something to be indifferently investigated. He returned three days running and covered a considerable amount of Ben Talbot's range. He found tracks by the dozen and several times he saw horsemen, usually in pairs or several riding together. He saw individual riders occasionally too, and went down to look for sign. There were always shod-horse tracks. Dozens of them.

It was this aspect that puzzled him the most. Not the rider as much as the fact that if he left tracks they were not distinctive.

There was an explanation, and there were many people around the territory who would have accepted it verbatim, but Sheriff Hall was not one of them. He did not believe in ghosts, phantoms, or any other kind of a rider who might have un-worldly attributes.

This was one reason why he did not talk about where he went riding nor what he was seeking out there even though several people in Bannonville were outspokenly interested in where the sheriff had been when it was expected he would be in town.

The situation changed. Ben Talbot's riders did not report any more sightings of the strange horseman. Springtime passed and summer arrived; people, particularly stockmen and others whose livelihoods depended on good weather, worked long hours. No one mentioned the horseman. Even when Sheriff Hall, whose persistence convinced him that there was a practical answer, visited the smithy and the corralyard to ascertain if either the yardboss or the blacksmith could elaborate on what they had told him earlier, both the blacksmith and the yardboss appeared uncomfortable and disinclined to discuss the subject, saying they were too busy.

Local people who had been intrigued by a phantom horseman earlier, and who had worked up some fascinating stories about him out of the whole cloth, were no longer interested. The subject had been worked to death, particularly since no additional sightings had been reported.

Sheriff Hall's curiosity lessened too, although he occasionally thought about the affair. It might in time have atrophied completely because, as was the case every summer, his duties kept him busy, particularly so on Saturday nights when rangemen converged from all directions on Bannonville. But a pot-hunter named Eliza Sharps walked into Hall's jailhouse office one summer evening, took a chair without saying a word, and appeared to be getting his thoughts organised as he eyed the gunrack across the room, then said, "Gettin' harder'n harder to find antelope any more. Deer too, but they ain't scarce they've just gone to the high country." Eliza paused, looked around, found no spittoon, leaned far over and let fly out the doorway. He straightened back and continued to gaze at the gunrack. "Bear's plentiful, but I have a hell of a time gettin' folks to buy the meat when I fetch it back down here."

Sheriff Hall drily said, "Can't imagine why, Eliza. Bears are carrion eaters, their meat don't smell good if it's covered with a tarp on a horse's back for a day or so."

The sarcasm went straight over the pothunter's head. He solemnly agreed with Hall. "I know it spoils fast, but I ain't got wings. I can't get down here with meat any faster'n my pack horse'll move, can I?"

Hall said, "No," and guessed the dilatory talk was about finished, but just in case it wasn't he helped it along with a question. "How are things back in the mountains?"

Eliza Sharps reached under his split-hide doeskin shirt to vigorously scratch while replying. "Well, like I said, it's gettin' harder to find meat, and there's somethin' else. Since the In'ians left I've had them mountains mostly to myself." Eliza stopped scratching, leaned again to expectorate, then went on as though there had been no little interruption. "Some days straight runnin' I come onto fresh camps up there. The stone rings was burnt, the ash was there, and at one camp there was horse droppings and sign of someone — just one someone — havin' been there not too long before."

"Another pot-hunter?"

"No. He didn't have no pack animal and his camp didn't show sign of trappings."

"A traveller, Eliza?"

Sharps's little pale eyes drifted slowly away from the gunrack to the sheriff's face. "Travellers travel. This feller made three camps no more'n about five miles apart over several days."

Sheriff Hall, who was a large, powerful man, greying and seasoned, a widower for seven years and with a wide acquaintanceship, studied the beard-stubbled, deeply lined and exposure-bronzed face of his visitor. "You got an idea?" he asked.

Sharps took his time about answering as he had taken his time about everything since he'd been a youngster of fifty. He was now seventy-five. He had to spray amber juice again before speaking. "A couple of things," he admitted. "One of 'em — at first camp he blanketed out his horse tracks. If I hadn't come onto the camp right soon after he'd left it, there wouldn't have been no sign to see. Just overnight dew or a littlest breeze'll flatten out sign that's been blanketed over."

Sheriff Hall went to the little iron office stove, poked kindling in, got a fire going and put his coffee-pot to heat. He returned to his chair and leaned both thick arms atop the desk.

"What else?" he asked.

"Nothing especially, Sheriff. Just that he don't belong in them mountains, so what's he doin' up there, shiftin' around back and forth as sneaky as a weasel, don't shoot no game, don't stay in one camp, drags out his sign?" Eliza Sharps's eyes remained unblinkingly on the sheriffs face. "Outlaw maybe? Renegade of some kind? It makes me a mite uneasy. I can find him an' I don't worry much about him findin' me, specially now that I know he's maybe still up there sneakin' around, so I camp in one of my secret places, but I ain't had to do that since the In'ians was taken away an' don't like doing it now."

Mark Hall went to check the coffee. It wasn't boiling-hot but it was hot enough so he drew off two cups and gave one to the older man, took the other cup to the desk with him, and during the little interlude while they both tested the liquid, he considered what he thought was a pretty good plan.

"Eliza, is he still up there?"

"I think so. I've been too busy tryin' to

12

find enough decent meat for town down here to worry much about him."

Hall sipped coffee for a moment. "He's got to know you're up there. If you're shooting game, sure as hell he's heard the shots."

Eliza held his cup away long enough to reply. "Not always, Sheriff. Unless he's scoutin' me up, because since he's been up there I been goin' miles easterly to hunt, and noise don't travel real good nor real far in a forest."

Hall put his cup aside. "Could you find him, Eliza?"

The older man scratched a stubbly cheek. "I expect so. I been doin' nothin' but huntin' for fifty years. A little more'n fifty in fact. First off, In'ians for the army, before that buffler." Sharps drained his cup and smiled at Sheriff Hall. "Folks look down their noses at me because I can't read nor write, an' I laugh to myself because I can track a fly across their windowpanes an' all they can do is read books." The older man looked steadily at Hall. "Why? If he's a renegade it's your job to find him, not mine."

Sheriff Hall did not dispute this. He said, "I can't read sign. If a track isn't set in soft ground I ride right by it. And I don't know the mountains."

"You've hunted 'em, Sheriff."

"Not the high country, only the lower-down places."

Sharps went to the stove, refilled his cup and returned to the chair. "It'll cut into my huntin' business."

Hall leaned back, fished for three silver cartwheels and put them on the edge of the desk. Eliza Sharps's claw-like hand closed around the money before it had cooled. He tucked it somewhere out of sight among his hide clothing and stood up. "I'll see what I can do," he said, and produced a soiled, limp scrap of brown paper which he put on Hall's desk. "That there is a map how to find my secret camp. You can use it if you don't hear from me within a couple of weeks. Maybe you'd better make it a mite longer. I never used to lose track

14

of days but I do now. Thanks for the coffee, Sheriff."

Hall spread out the paper. It had been meticulously drawn by someone whose inability to write descriptions had been effectively overcome by his ability to draw trees, big rocks, trails and waterways.

The sheriff was lighting his lamp when it occurred to him that drawing that map had been real labour for the old pot-hunter. It also occurred to him that since Eliza had drawn that map before meeting the sheriff, he'd planned everything in advance.

Hall laughed aloud. That damned old screwt had perfected his plan all the time he was riding down out of the mountains. He'd figured out a way to compensate for the scarcity of game by getting Hall sufficiently interested to pay him to hunt down the stranger.

What Eliza did not know, could not have known, was that everything he had told Mark Hall fitted into the earlier mystery of the disappearing horseman.

2

A Surprise

SUMMER days were long. Animals, human and other, had something like ten hours of sunlight, more than most of them needed for making a living, which left three or four more hours of daylight to use for other things.

Ben Talbot met Sheriff Hall at the Bannonville saloon one Saturday evening with a tale of dying cattle. It had taken Ben three days to figure out what was happening, by which time he'd found eleven carcasses within a mile or two of a particular sump spring.

He told the sheriff he still didn't know what had caused those deaths, not the basic reason anyway, but after he and his riders had worked from dawn until dusk setting posts and stringing wire so cattle could not drink at that place, there

16

had been no more deaths.

They had a drink together, agreed that hot weather made scum on troughs and at still-water springs and ponds, decided the stagnant water had been responsible for the dead cattle, and had another drink when Ben changed the topic and said, "Did you know Charley Silver? He owned a few thousand acres south of here about fifteen miles. Old feller, ran maybe three hundred cows, drove everywhere in a wagon because of back trouble."

Hall knew the old man. "To nod to is about all. He didn't come to town often. What about him?"

"Some son of a bitch drygulched him."

Hall's eyes widened. "Killed him?"

"Deader'n a stone, Mark. A couple of my riders were combing-out down there and saw the wagon. Old Charley'd been dead a couple of days. Shot through the heart from in back. I went down there with the crew and buried him. We left the wagon where it happened and threw the harness in the back." Talbot leaned

17

on the bar looking at his whiskey glass. "I knew Charley pretty well. Knew him most of my life in fact. He'd been married once. His wife died. She's buried out there somewhere. He wouldn't say where." Talbot continued to regard the whiskey glass, which was empty. "A man don't always get neighbours he likes, but Charley wasn't like that at all. He'd bend over backwards to be a good neighbour. I hadn't seen him for a couple of years but when I was a lot younger he was like an uncle to me."

Talbot turned to look at Mark Hall. "I can't figure it out. I been thinking about it ever since, and damned if I can come up with a single reason why anyone would want old Charley dead."

Hall asked a question. "Is the wagon still out there where he got shot?"

"As far as I know it is. We sure didn't move it. But I haven't been back down there. I'm awful busy this time of year and it's a long ride."

Hall poured them both another jolt. "I'll ride down there," he said, and

18

Talbot nodded his head. "I'd take it kindly, Mark."

But it was three days before Sheriff Hall could shake loose for the ride. He started out before sun-up. A thirty miles ride going and coming used up a long day, even if a man didn't spend some time scouting around.

He found the wagon without difficulty because Charley Silver's range was mostly as flat as the palm of a man's hand, some of the best grassland in the country. Sheriff Hall passed several bands of sassy-fat calves and their mammies who were as slick as moles.

There was dried blood on the wagonseat, down in the boot, and up along the wooden dashboard. There was blood beneath the wagon too where it had dripped through cracks in the floorboards.

Sheriff Hall finished examining the wagon and leaned in hot sunlight studying the roundabout country. There were some erosion washes, not very deep and mostly grassed over so that additional rains would not widen or deepen them.

There were no trees within a mile of the wagon, and there was no sign of big rocks, of the kind that existed a few miles farther northward where they were indifferently spread over miles of range country, perfect for ambushes, but not down where the old cowman had been killed.

Sheriff Hall rode slowly in the direction of the Silver house, barn and ranch yard. Long before he got there he could sense the utter stillness, complete silence of the place. It made hair rise on the back of his neck.

He tied up at the barn, loosened the cinch and went over to the house. Inside, it looked exactly the way someone might have left it. There were breakfast dishes on the kitchen table, a two-thirds empty whiskey jug on a wooden drainboard, and some long out-dated old newspapers near a chair in the parlour where a table and coal-oil lamp stood close. There was even a pair of steel-rimmed eyeglasses on the little table.

Hall prowled through the house. It

had five rooms but one door was locked. It had been old Charley's wife's sewing-room and probably had not been opened or aired out since her death years before.

The bedroom which had obviously been used most had bedclothes tossed back as would have been the case if someone had arisen with the intention of perhaps returning later to make the bed.

There was on old rolltop desk in a corner piled indifferently with papers. A bottom desk drawer was half open, as though Charley had carelessly left it like that when he'd left the bedroom.

There were several guns; one near the kitchen door leading into the yard, probably for varmints, another one to one side of the front door, a long-barrelled old hunting gun on pegs above the stone fireplace. It had a bird's eye stock of some pale wood and looked perfectly preserved. There were also several handguns. One was hanging on the back of the kitchen door in a holster which was suspended from an old, stained shellbelt which had only about a dozen bullets in its loops.

Mark Hall went down to the barn. The stalls were empty, as were the corrals out back. He watered his animal, snugged up the cinch and left the yard on an angling course for Bannonville.

By the time he had rooftops in sight, although it was still daylight there were shadows forming miles northward where virgin timber stood in ranks all the way to timber-line, beyond which nothing grew and dirty ice remained in cracks and crevices near the topouts.

Old Eliza was up there somewhere.

Sheriff Hall left his horse with the liveryman, went over to the cafe to eat, and when all the pleats had been ironed out of his belly, he crossed to the jailhouse, parked his coat and hat, sat down and meticulously rolled a cigarette.

He had kept his word to Ben Talbot. He had gone down to the Silver place. He had used up a very long day, had covered about thirty miles, and — as he

22

lit up — told himself that he did not know a damned bit more now than he had known before he'd left town this morning.

Over the years Sheriff Hall had encountered maybe more than his share of unresolved murders. It was one of the exasperations of his line of work that successes were nowhere nearly as commonplace as folks thought they were.

He drank a little cold coffee because it was hot enough in his office without adding to that by firing up the stove, and he rolled another smoke.

There was a reason. There had to be a reason, even in nine-tenths of the unsolved murders there had to have been a reason for the killings.

He tipped ash, arose stiffly to light the coal-oil lamp which hung suspended from the ceiling by a length of wire, and went back to his desk to stub out the smoke and lean back far enough to be able to prop his booted feet atop the desk.

He recalled everything he could

remember about Charley Silver, and failed to come up with enemies, or any other reason why someone would bushwhack him.

There were just two things he kept coming back to, and neither of them had a hell of a lot to do with the murder. Not as far as Mark Hall could see, anyway.

One of them was that it seemed that Talbot had said old Charley had been dead for a couple of days down there in his wagon, and when Ben and his crew had returned a couple of days later to bury him, they'd turned the team loose. Maybe he hadn't said that but it seemed like he had.

Maybe Ben hadn't gotten that right. Most likely he'd been so upset he hadn't meant that when *he* went back they turned the horses loose; maybe he meant that when his *riders* found old Charley they had freed the hitch.

But that wasn't really the problem. Anybody knew that harness horses or even saddle animals would get hungry, thirsty, and downright restless if they had to stand around for just one day, and a team on a wagon with a dead man in it, no hand to hold them back, no foot to kick on the binders, would stand around just so long, then they'd start grazing along pulling the wagon with them.

The other nagging little item was that half-closed bottom drawer in old Charley's desk. Maybe it was nothing. Most likely it didn't amount to a damn, but if there was a reason for the killing, it could easily have had something to do with money, most killings did have, and if old Charley kept a pouch of gold coins or cartwheels in that drawer . . .

Sheriff Hall swore at himself for not having opened the drawer wider to look into it.

He speculated about the bushwhacker. Hell, this time of year with the cow outfits hard at it using strangers no one knew anything about, not to mention the steady stream of other strangers passing through, some on the stages, some in wagons, many on horseback, trying to find one suspicious stranger would be like looking for a needle in a haystack.

It would not now be possible to examine Charley's fatal wound either. But if the slug had come from one of the standard range weapons, all anyone would be able to determine was that a murder had been committed by someone who owned the kind of weapon everyone else owned.

The Bannonville gunsmith, a grizzled, short, burly man named Ike Cameron, drifted in because he had noticed the light from across in front of the general store, and because he and Sheriff Hall went back a long ways.

"Are you just settin' here," the gunsmith asked drily, "or are you glued to that chair?"

Hall's gaze went to the older man's face and remained there. "Did you know Charley Silver?"

"*Did* I know him? You mean he isn't any more?"

"Someone bushwhacked him. Killed him."

26

The gunsmith's eyes widened in shock. "Charley Silver? He never made an enemy in his life."

"I don't know. That's what I was doing when you walked in; trying to figure it out. Ben Talbot's riders found him. They buried him a few days ago."

Ike Cameron, who had walked in with some idea in mind of swapping behind-the-barn jokes with the sheriff, sat motionless for a long time. "Was he robbed? Did someone drive off his cattle or horses?"

Hall put a wry look on the gunsmith. "I told you, Ike. I don't know what happened. I just know he was killed. But I didn't see the body. All I found was the wagon where it happened."

Cameron began to solemnly nod his head. "Rustlers sure as hell. If you go down there you're goin' to find his cattle are all gone. Maybe his horses too." He raised his eyes to the sheriff's face, missed seeing the pained expression, and shoved up out of the chair as he spoke. "It had to be something like that.

I've known Charley Silver more years than I want to look back on, and for a fact, Sheriff, I've yet to hear anyone say anything bad about him."

Hall watched the gunsmith go back out into the darkness. Nobody had to say anything bad about Silver, all they'd had to do was draw a bead on him from in back.

Sheriff Hall had once heard a man say that among Americans it was a smart individual who knew who his grandfather was, and among Frenchmen it was a smart man who knew who his father was.

It occurred to Mark Hall that that feller should have added another sentence: it was a smart man who knew who his enemies were.

He put out the lamp, locked the jailhouse from the roadway, and went along to the house he now lived in alone, but about which he had told himself many times over the past seven years, he had lived the happiest, most wonderful years of his life.

3

A Sighting

SHERRIFF HALL returned to the Charley Silver place, curious about whether others might have been there since his last visit.

Word of the killing had of course spread, and in its wake there was considerable indignation. Mark Hall wanted to see if that indignation had been from the heart, or whether it might not have masked someone's real purpose — looting — and if so if perhaps the looter might not have left more evidence of his presence than Charley's assassin had, unless they were the same person.

The sheriff was grasping at straws and would have been the first to admit it, but the alternative was to do nothing, which would rankle around town and would also trouble Mark Hall.

He left town in pitch dark and arrived northeast of Charley's yard as the sun was rising. He dismounted out a fair distance and squatted in damp grass waiting for sunlight to brighten the yard. He chose his point of vantage well. He had a stand of jack-pines at his back and for several yards on both sides, and he had kept those trees between himself and the yard on his approach. If he had been moving after sunrise it was possible someone would have noticed. He had arrived down here before sunrise and was now in place as motionless as a stone. Someone might still detect his presence but nowhere nearly as readily as they otherwise could have.

He watched as newday light heightened a number of square outlines. Of the house, the barn, several small outbuildings and the dug-well which was close to the front veranda to the east, not far from the kitchen door.

He had that same odd feeling of uneasiness because of the utter stillness and seemingly depthless silence down there. If he'd been superstitious he would have wondered if perhaps those things didn't mean a haunting.

A foraging dog-coyote appeared around the east side of the house where he stopped and tested the air before trotting directly across the yard, something a coyote would rarely do if he'd detected any fresh human scent.

Mark Hall sighed to himself. There was no one down there. But he continued to sit in tree camouflage. There would be plenty of time to see if the house had been looted after he was satisfied no one was going to show up.

He badly needed a suspect.

But unless he wanted to apprehend that foraging coyote it did not appear he was going to catch anyone, so he mounted, reined clear of the trees and started for the yard.

Down there, with erect hair on the back of his neck, he stalled his horse and went over to the house.

It had been some time since Charley Silver had been there. The varmints

31

people kept at bay during a residency but which stubbornly continued to exist barely beyond shooting range, and which inched their way back when they could detect no resistance, had been at work in Charley's house. A wood rat had half a constructed nest in the kitchen woodbox and smaller creatures including one bold small wren, had achieved access and were busily taking over in the parlour.

Sheriff Hall's first step on the front porch sent all those creatures fleeing, but after he entered at least a half-dozen little beady black eyes watched everything he did from several secret places.

Hall heard little rustling sounds as he stood in the centre of the parlour. As far as he could determine, nothing was missing. Even that valuable old long-rifle above the fireplace was still up there.

In the bedroom everything appeared the same, even that half-open bottom desk drawer.

There was probably an infinite variety of things mice, rats and wrens would find a use for, eventually including that half-open drawer, but so far there were no such signs.

Mark leaned, carefully opened the drawer and found it empty. Other drawers had things in them, papers, odds and ends, faded newspapers going back many years. A few opened letters still in their envelopes. Nearly every drawer was too full to accommodate much more, except that empty lower one, but that didn't have to mean anything.

He straightened up, looking around for footprints in the dust. There were some, mostly his own footprints. He thought there was another set made by a smaller boot, but when he found one of Charley's old boots and placed it in the track it fitted perfectly.

But someone had been here after the sheriff had. They had probably been here earlier too, perhaps within hours after Charley was killed. There were signs of a meal having been prepared and eaten between the sheriffs first visit down here and his present visit.

Out in the parlour he built and lit

a smoke, felt annoyed with himself for not having camped down here for a few days after the killing and went to the murky front window to stand wide-legged staring northward.

There was a solitary horseman sitting sideways looking toward the yard from what appeared to be about a half-mile northward. Under the newday sun's brilliance he seemed to be riding, or at least sitting on, a black horse. Neither the animal nor the man moved as Mark's cigarette went out between his lips and those neck hairs arose again.

He left the house with a thrusting stride, heading for the barn. Down there, he led his horse out, snugged up the cinch, put on the bridle and led his animal outside to be mounted.

The horseman was no longer up there. The land was as empty as it usually was.

The sheriff turned his head very slowly, blocking in all the country he could see from the yard. It was open, with some arroyos but they did not appear as anything other than flat terrain until someone rode up to them, at which time he could look down into them. But to Frank Hall's knowledge none of those gullies was deep enough to conceal a mounted man.

He was turning to mount when a keening high yell sounded from the southwest where a pair of rangemen were loping toward the yard. Hall hesitated, watched the loping horsemen for a moment, looked northward again where there was no movement of any kind, and rose up to settle in his saddle as the loping riders reached the western rim of the big yard and called to him.

One of them was holding a carbine in his lap. Neither of them raised a hand in the customary palm-outward sign of greeting.

Hall reached to tug loose the thong that held his sidearm in its holster then placed both hands on the saddlehorn and studied the riders. Both were young, neither one carried any excess weight, one had straw-coloured hair showing

35

beneath his sweat-stained dark hat and the other man was dark, perhaps with the kind of oily skin that darkened from long exposure to the sun. He had startlingly blue eyes.

He saw the lighter one say something from the corner of his mouth and guessed they had noticed the badge on his shirt. He was correct. When they came up and halted, both men smiled and the dark man up-ended his Winchester and slid it back into its boot as the light-haired man said, "'Morning, Sheriff. We seen you crossin' toward the barn from out a ways but didn't know who it was."

Hall thought that was as close to an apology for making a run on him with a weapon showing as he was going to get, and asked a question.

"Did you see anyone else?"

The two rangeriders looked bemused before the dark man answered. "There wasn't no one else. Just you."

Hall leaned on his saddlehorn. "When you were out yonder could you see northward around the barn?"

The dark man bobbed his head. "Yeah. That's what we was doing. Watchin' up there and all around. We work for Mister van der Work, the feller who bought two ranches south of here. He's been bringin' in bred-up redbacks an' they drift to beat hell."

Sheriff Hall had been a rangeman himself. He knew about drifting cattle, especially this time of year when there was feed everywhere, and especially when cattle were new in a country.

He changed the subject. "Don't believe I know Mister van der Work."

The cowboys slouched as the light-haired man lifted his hat, combed his mane with a set of bent fingers, replaced the hat and smiled. "He come into the country about a year back. We rode for Arledge and Mason. When Mister van der Work bought both ranches he kept us on. He kept on all the riders and commenced sending up quality cattle. We got close to two thousand head now." The blond man's smile widened, a bit wryly. "And he's still sendin' them."

Sheriff Hall nodded. "Which ranch does he stay at?"

"Neither of 'em," the blond man said, shifting his weight in the saddle. "He lives down in Denver. He comes up now an' then."

Absentee owners were no novelty to Sheriff Hall. "Does he have a rangeboss?"

"Yeah. Feller named Morgan Trevithick. He hired him somewhere else. Morgan don't know this country any better'n the other couple of fellers Mister van der Work sent up from Denver to work for him."

Mark Hall went to work fashioning a smoke and until he had lighted up nothing more was said. He had taken this conversation about as far as it was going to go, so he smiled as he said, "I guess you boys knew Charley Silver."

Both men nodded and the dark man wagged his head. "That's the damndest thing. I've been workin' in this country off an' on for about eight years. I knew Charley pretty well." The dark man wagged his head again and lapsed into solemn silence.

Hall killed his smoke atop the saddle-horn. "I came out to look around," he told them as he raised his rein-hand. "A long ride for nothing, I guess."

They said nothing so he nodded, reined around and left the yard riding north. The cowboys sat in the yard watching him depart. When he was about where he had seen the man on the black horse they turned back the way they had come, with Silver's log barn obscuring their view northward, up where Sheriff Hall was riding leaning slightly from the saddle looking for tracks.

There were none. There was trampled grass in all directions made by cattle grazing through. It was impossible to separate one set of marks from another. Moreover, the grass was lush, matted and had been dew-soaked the night before. Hall looked back, did not see the riders until they emerged on the south side of the barn talking back and forth and without even glancing up where Hall was riding.

He spat, said a hair-raising word and set his course for Bannonville. He'd never in his life wanted to be an Indian, but right now he'd have given six months of his wages to be able to read sign like Indians could.

He knew what he had seen out there. He was also perfectly satisfied that the man on the black horse had left tracks. This time, unlike Ben Talbot's experience under similar circumstances, there were tracks. He just could not make them out.

He was half-way to town when it occurred to him that perhaps all those cattle tracks in the wet grass were not the result of just cattle grazing through. Someone could have driven them past the yard northward.

But what in hell for? No one had known Sheriff Hall was going to ride down there this morning. He hadn't told a soul.

There was another reason to suspect

he was getting a mite troubled in the head about all this. He had encountered bands of old Charley's animals with his big CS brand a mile or two north and east of the yard. They could have been the same critters who had grazed through last night, or maybe last evening just before night fell.

He stopped at a little cold-water creek to tank up his horse, stand in willow-shade gazing far and wide with only the barest of hopes that he might see the man on the black horse again.

He didn't.

There was an accumulation of fluffy white clouds coming in from the east by the time he reached town, left his animal with the liveryman and went up to the office. If those clouds ganged all together, it might rain. The land did not particularly need a downpour, although no livestockman would agree with that. They never agreed with something like that. Not even a couple of days after the last downpour.

The sheriff went after his bottle of

corn liquor in the store-room, put it upon the desk, tossed aside his hat and coat, sat down and stared at the bottle.

That son of a bitch had been out there!

He reached for the bottle, tipped back his chair and swallowed twice, and because he had not eaten since last night, the effects were almost immediate.

He fumbled around putting the bottle in a lower drawer of his desk, straightened up to regard the hanging-lamp in the middle of the room and rubbed his eyes, swore when there appeared to still be more than one lamp, and shook his head.

He had been hungry when he had ridden into the alley behind the livery barn. He probably still was hungry, but he was far less conscious of it now.

He drank what was left of cold black coffee in the office pot, groped for his hat and went out into the fragrant, soft summer dusk.

Across the road people were entering and departing at the cafe. It was the height of supper-time. He did not cross over, he instead turned in the direction of the rooming-house where he lived, and where he could, upon rare occasions, talk the landlady into feeding him.

She would know he had a load on, and she would probably scold him, but that was better than appearing over at the cafe with eyes that wouldn't focus when the place was full of people who knew from experience when someone had a load on.

43

4

Sherriff Hall's Visitor

HER name was Helen Mosley. She was buxom, had green eyes and coppery hair, was several years older than the sheriff, and had inherited the rooming-house from her brother, who had never married. She had been married but had also been widowed.

When the sheriff walked into her kitchen she brushed back a heavy coil of hair, opened her mouth to speak, then slowly closed it and pointed to a chair at an oilcloth-covered circular table as she scathingly said, "Why don't you eat first? A man your age should know better. In the morning you're going to feel like hell."

Sheriff Hall smiled weakly as he watched her go to the stove and fill a bowl with the one thing he would always associate with Helen Mosley: barley soup made the way no one else on earth could make it. "I forgot to eat," he told her, and flinched under the bleak glare she put on him as she turned from the stove with his steaming bowl.

She put it in front of him, put down a large spoon and said, "Eat. All of it. I'll make some fresh coffee."

"Helen, You're — "

"Yes, I know. I'm sweeter than molasses, prettier than a speckled pony, and am the best cook on earth. Mark Hall, a man in your position should never get drunk."

"I'm not drunk. Just took a couple of swallows on an empty stomach."

She went on as though he had not spoken. "In your line of work you need your wits about you all the time. You can't afford not to be co-ordinated and alert."

She filled his cup then got one for herself and took it to the table where she sat opposite him watching the large spoon rise and fall with an almost pendulum-like precision. When the bowl was empty she would have refilled it but he put a massive palm over it and shook his head at her.

He had begun feeling better shortly after he'd started to eat. Now, he no longer had anything remotely like double vision. Even the bone-weariness from a long day of saddlebacking had departed. He smiled broadly at her. "If you ever sell this place," he told her, "and move to China, when you open your door the next morning I'll be on your doorstep."

She seemed to be wistful, but only for a very brief moment. "Go to bed, Mark."

He seemed agreeable to that suggestion but continued to sit gazing across the table at her. "Did you know Charley Silver?"

"Yes. Several times he'd lie over in town and I'd rent him a room. And I heard what happened to him." Her green eyes widened a degree as she stared across the table. "Is that where you were today, at his ranch?"

"Yeah. Left town in the wee hours

on an empty stomach, spent some time down there and didn't get back to town until dusk. On an empty stomach."

She ignored his emphasis on the empty stomach, leaned on the table with knitted brows and said, "Who killed him? What did you find down there?"

"Not much. A couple of cowboys who were hunting cattle. They work for someone named van der Work who bought two ranches south of Charley." He paused to lean back, looking steadily at her. "Have you heard the story that's been goin' around town about a phantom horseman?"

She had indeed heard the stories. She had also made about the same judgment Sheriff Hall had made. "The way I heard it, only two people from town have really seen him, the corralyard boss and the blacksmith. But there seems to be fifty who haven't see him who are telling all the stories." She looked steadily at Mark Hall for a moment, then leaned back off the table with a troubled brow. "You saw him?"

"As clear as I see you right this minute."

"Did you go after him?"

"Couldn't right away. Those cowboys stopped me. But when I got out there he was gone and I'm not a good-enough sign reader to have found his tracks."

"What would he be doing down at Charley Silver's place?" she asked, and made the sheriff sit opposite her, staring owlishly for a long moment before he said, "Yeah. What was he doing down at the Silver place?"

She was beginning to have second thoughts. "Are you sure you didn't have something to drink down there?"

He felt colour coming into his face. "I told you — I didn't have anything all day but a drink of creek-water on the way back. Helen, I know what I saw!"

She reached for her cup. "Mark, I don't think I'd tell anyone else about it, if I were you."

He continued to glare at her, then threw up his hands, shoved up to his feet and thanked her from the heart, with just the slightest hint of brusqueness, before walking to the swinging door. He was raising a hand to push when she spoke.

"I believe you. I also believe something else."

He turned, waiting.

She smiled up at him. She was a handsome woman. Her smile enhanced it, at least to Sheriff Hall. "I don't believe he is a myth or a phantom, and Mark — why would he have killed Charley?"

Hall's thoughts were scattered. He forgot about the door at his back. "Who said he did?"

"No one. Nor did I say it. But why would he have, if he did, and why was he down there today?"

Hall let his breath out in a long sigh. "Helen, I don't know very much about any of this, but I'm goin' to try my damndest to find out."

She smiled very sweetly. "And you'll tell me, Mark?"

He didn't say whether he would or

not. He said, "You sure have pretty eyes," and pushed on out of the kitchen heading for his room and his bed.

He was exhausted, as full of barley soup as a tick, weary clean through to the bone, and he lay there staring at the ceiling trying to imagine why that man on the black horse might have shot Charley Silver in the back. *If* he had done that to old Charley. And whether he had or not, what had he been doing down yonder today, out in plain sight like he wanted to be seen?

The mysterious rider invoked more questions than a man could answer in hours. Mark Hall fell asleep not even half-way through enumerating them.

The following morning while he was over at the general store buying a sack of Durham and some wheatstraw papers, a birdlike elderly soul Hall had never seen before walked up to him and smilingly said, "Sheriff Hall, I'll be over in your office," and walked out of the store with both Hall and the bald storekeeper staring after him. The storekeeper said,

"Undertaker, sure as hell."

The storekeeper wasn't even close. The man gave his name as Albert George, his business as abstracts, land titles, mortgages and anything that had to do with land and title to it. He told Sherriff Hall that Charley Silver had died without heirs, that a full search had turned up the fact that Charley and his late wife'd had no issue, and as far as Mister Albert George could determine after a very extensive hunt, neither Charley nor his wife had any living kin.

Mark Hall had known none of this, had not thought about any of it, but he knew what happened in cases like this so he said, "Then the ranch and livestock go to the state," and the wispy little birdlike man smiled with twinkling eyes as he said, "Yes, normally that's the procedure."

Sheriff Hall leaned forward on his desk. "But not this time, Mister George?"

"Oh yes indeed, Sheriff Hall. Yes indeed. When it was shown that the unfortunate Mister Silver had no heirs, his holdings were deeded to the state."

Hall leaned back slowly. "He's only been dead about three weeks, maybe a month, Mister George."

The elderly man removed rimless glasses and vigorously polished them on a white handkerchief before speaking again. He kept squinting at the polished glasses, not at Sheriff Hall. "I started my searching quite early. It didn't take as long as most searches require." Mister George hooked the glasses back into place, looked through them at Mark Hall and smiled pleasantly. "I'm efficient, Sheriff. When a man works for himself he has to be." Mister George hung fire briefly and swung his attention to the gunrack on the distant wall. "These things have to be advertised in the newspaper. The law requires as much. I can assure you, Sheriff, every legal requirement has been complied with."

The sheriff leaned forward again, very slowly this time, gazing steadily at the older man. He placed both elbows atop the desk and leaned his chin on them. He was beginning to have an uncomfortable feeling, rather like a bad premonition. He quietly said, "What's the rest of it?"

Albert George moved his stare from the far wall to the little pot-bellied iron stove and kept it there. "Well, everything was done legally. No heirs were located. Advertisements were posted, the Silver place and its chattels were deeded to the state, and sold."

Sheriff Hall did not seem to be breathing. He had gone through this same procedure several times when people had died without anyone being able to locate heirs, but it had required a lot more time than a month. It had required a year just to be sure no heir was going to show up, and after that, when land had been sold, it had been done so with a provision that it could be redeemed within three years. Not months, years.

The sheriff said, "Sold?"

"Yes. Sold."

"Who was it sold to, Mister George?"

The sinewy older man fished around in his coat until he located some impressive-appearing legal papers and re-set his glasses after unfolding them. "Yes. Here it is. It was sold . . . Are you interested in the exact date and time, Sheriff?"

"No."

Albert George cleared his throat. He was nervous. "It was sold to a Mister Henry van der Work of Denver."

Mister George folded the papers, pocketed them and finally looked over where Sheriff Hall was sitting like a burly Buddha looking back. Mister George looked quickly away, smoothed his trousers, stood up and shot another look toward the desk. "What I have here are copies of the original legal documents. The originals are to be recorded in Denver. Probably by now they've already been recorded . . . Sheriff?"

Mark Hall arose. "One question, Mister George. All that's required is that the transfer of title to the new owner be recorded. Why did you come down here to Bannonville and look me up?"

The elderly man was adjusting his coat when he replied. "It was thought that if you understood the status of the Silver ranch, you'd be able to satisfy local opinion. You know how it is in these distant cattle towns, Sheriff. People can be interested in a ranch with cattle on it when they know the owner is dead. Sometimes with an idea to acquiring the place, and perhaps more often with some idea of looting it, running off some cattle, stealing a few horses . . . "

"And what you're beating around the bush about, Mister George, is that someone wants the local law to make sure none of these things happen."

Albert George ran a bony finger around under his collar. He felt very intimidated, not just by Mark Hall's size, but by his almost silken-soft way of speaking which did not match the steely gaze from his eyes. "Yes, something like that, Sheriff . . . Mister van der Work's newest holding does lie within your jurisdiction, doesn't it?"

Hall did not answer. He walked around from behind his desk and smiled down into the slight, older man's shiny face. "One more question, if you don't mind, Mister George."

"No, of course I don't mind."

"Do you personally know Henry van der Work?"

"I've met him, yes. After all, that couldn't have been avoided, could it? He required the title and inheritance search."

"An' he hired you to do those things for him?"

"Yes."

"So you know him personally," said Sheriff Hall, his smile fading, his steely look more noticeable, "and he hired you to make everything legal, and unless I'm wrong as hell the only way you could have done all that searching and filing and whatnot, you'd have to have started on it at least a couple of months ago."

"It does indeed take time, Sheriff," the older man said a little breathlessly.

Hall nodded slowly. "You want to

know what I think, you little weasel?"

Mister George recoiled a step before what probably appeared to him as imminent violence. "Sheriff, I have a job to do. You know that."

"I think, Mister George, that to get all that letter-writing done, and all the answering letters back, and all the title-searching done and the filing and all, that you had to have started on it about a month before Charley Silver was killed."

Mister Albert groped behind him for the wall. What his hand encountered was the roadway door. It was ajar and as he gripped it, the door swung wide open. When he was in the doorway Mister George said, "If I was you, Sheriff, I'd be very careful about saying things like that. Everything was done legally. That was what Mister van der Work wanted . . . I won't mention what you just said, Sheriff. Good day to you."

Mister George nearly fell in his haste to reach the walkway. He went hurriedly northward up out of Mark Hall's sight.

He had already paid for a seat on the evening stage going north out of Bannonville. He had done what he had been sent down to do. He had been worried from the moment he stepped into the first southbound stage on the long journey down to Bannonville. He was no longer worried. He had done his job and, as he would reflect later, he had done it quite well.

He was no longer worried, he was frightened half to death. No one had told him in Denver what kind of a man the sheriff of Fancher County was.

Long before the northbound stage out of Bannonville was ready to roll, he had made a firm resolution never again to hire out his services to Henry van der Work, whether or not he was one of the wealthiest and, so it was said, most politically powerful men west of the Missouri river.

5

Beginning the Groundwork

SHERRIFF HALL had a mid-day meal in a sour frame of mind, and later, when he was standing in front of the jailhouse and saw the northbound stage leave town, he watched its progress until it was partially obscured by dust, then went over to the general store, which was also the local post office and had a number of little box-like squares nailed to a wall, like pigeon nests, where letters were stuffed in until called for, and cornered the beefy, bald storekeeper to ask a question.

"Did you know a feller from Denver bought the Arledge and Mason ranches south of town?"

The bald man nodded. "Yeah. I guess everyone around town knows it."

"So neither Mason nor Arledge get

mail here any more?"

"That's right. Neither one of 'em does. I heard that Dick Arledge went out to California and Johnny Mason — "

"Yeah. Went to Texas. What I'd like to know is who is getting whatever mail comes along for the man who now owns those ranches."

The bald man spread thick hands atop the counter and leaned on them. "No one gets mail down at those places, Mark. There ain't been a letter in here for anyone down there since that Denver-feller bought the ranches."

As the lawman's partly puzzled, partly annoyed look registered with the merchant over a long moment of silence, he turned and pointed to one of the pigeon nests where a letter had been placed and said, "That there box is the only new one in six months. That letter's been there for five weeks. I don't do a hell of a lot of mail business. It's sort of a convenience, an' it makes folks come to the store." The bald man smiled self-consciously. "Runnin' a store makes a man lie awake nights figuring ways to increase his volume. You understand."

Sheriff Hall nodded indifferently. "Yeah," he said and left the building.

He went up to the saloon, bought a glass of tepid beer and leaned on the counter nursing it while gazing off into space. It was a slack time of day for the saloonman, who leaned against his backbar eyeing Sheriff Hall with a discerning gaze. In the saloonman's business a person developed an intuitive sixth sense about customers, not to mention a capacity for tact that would have made a politician proud.

When Hall drained the glass the saloonman reached for it as he said, "Refill? Somethin' botherin' you, Sheriff?"

Hall's gaze went to the man's jowly face. "Yes, somethin' is botherin' me. In fact a lot of things are botherin' me."

The saloonman had great respect for Sheriff Hall, who had cracked heads and put down near riots in his place of business over the years. "Anythin' I can help with?" he asked.

Mark Hall started to shake his head, then said, "You heard a feller from Denver bought a couple of ranches south of town about fifteen, twenty miles?"

The barman had indeed heard. He even knew the buyer's name. "Yeah. I guess a lot of folks around town have heard that. The buyer's name is van der Work. That's a name folks aren't likely to forget real easy. What kind of a name is it, do you know?"

Sheriff Hall shook his head; he didn't know and he didn't care. "Do his riders visit your saloon?"

The barman shrugged beefy shoulders. "This time of year there are more strangers around town than you can shake a stick at. I don't know who they ride for." The barman paused, eyed the sheriff briefly then leaned and said, "I could find out, I think. You want me to let you know?"

Hall smiled for the first time today as he pulled back from the counter. "I'd appreciate it," he said, and walked out of the saloon.

He was down at the jailhouse with his feet on the desk, his chair tipped perilously back, when an unshaven, gaunt old left-over from earlier days filled his doorway, gazed steadily at the sheriff, and without a word walked to a chair and sat down. His perpetually narrowed eyes roamed the room as he said, "Don't look like you folks got any rain down here. We sure got a drenching in the mountains." The pale eyes came around to Mark Hall's face and settled there. They had a sardonic look to them. "Normally, I ain't fond of cloudbursts but nowadays with game gettin' harder to find, it sure helps. I tracked some wapiti up under the rims, shot four fat yearling bucks, an' just finished puttin' them into the storekeeper's icehouse out back. He paid me cash."

Sheriff Hall remained silent and tilted back as he studied old Eliza Sharps.

Old Eliza briefly sucked his teeth, then let his eyes wander again. "I found him. I could have stoled his black horse and set him afoot up where he'd be a week findin' his way out."

Hall's feet came down off the desk as he leaned on the desk. "Who is he?"

"Don't know, exactly, but I can tell you a little about him. When he leaves he don't come back for several days. He wears an ivory-stocked sixgun an his Winchester's got one of those ivory front-sights for night-shooting. He's middlin' young. Maybe thirty, thirty-five, sort of tall, not fat anywhere, an' you know how I come onto him? He plays a mouth organ. The sound don't travel far up there among the trees, but it carries some. And he plays real nice. I lay hid in the weeds one evenin' listenin' for an hour."

Sheriff Hall examined a hangnail before digging out his clasp-knife to work on it with. "Think back," he said, while preparing to cut the hangnail. "Think back about three weeks, Eliza."

Sharps groaned. "Three weeks back don't mean anythin' to me. No more'n last week or next week."

Hall finished whittling, returned the

64

knife to his pocket and looked at the old pot-hunter. "All right. Let's try it another way. Since the last full moon has he been gone from his camp?"

Eliza had no difficulty with this at all. "Yes sir, he has. About the time of the new moon. He was gone for a couple of days."

Hall relaxed, leaned to grope for his bottle of malt whiskey and put it within the old man's reach. Eliza tipped his head, blew out a fiery breath and put the bottle back on the desk. "Much obliged," he said, wiping his eyes on a greasy doeskin cuff. "By gawd that's good whiskey, Sheriff."

"When you go take the bottle with you, if you want it, Eliza. But be careful. That stuffs got a kick like an army mule."

"Thank you, Mister Hall. I'll drink to your health when I get back home."

The liquor worked rather quickly, possibly because the old man had not had any in a long time, or perhaps because being older than dirt, he did not have the tolerance to hard liquor he once might have had. It hit him the way it hit Irishmen and Indians; immediately and with a predictable result. He became talkative.

"Tell you what I think, Sheriff. I think the son of a bitch is a fugitive. Maybe a bank robber or a stage robber. Something like that. An' from time to time he sneaks out to see if there's a posse searchin' around for him."

Hall leaned back again. "Maybe," he conceded. "Do you have a mirror, Eliza?"

"Steel one I stole from the army years back."

"Do you know what heliographing is?"

Sharps snorted, and had to rummage for an old blue bandana to dab at his nose with before replying. "Sheriff I was heliographin' with a steel mirror while they was still stuffin' your three-cornered pants with absorbent moss."

Mark Hall grinned. "You most likely were." He dug in a pocket, brought forth three silver cartwheels, placed them beside the bottle and said, "Next time he leaves the uplands, find a place where someone down here can see up there, and flash your steel mirror four times, lay back a while then four more times. Can you do it?"

Sharps was leaning toward the silver dollars without taking his pale eyes off Mark Hall when he answered. "Did I tell you I never learned to read nor write? Well, but the army taught me how to send certain flashes for certain marks they made on a paper. They taught me how to string them marks together. It made words scouts could decipher fifty miles away. I remember them marks. You write some on a paper and I'll send you a full message in flashes from up yonder."

Mark Hall laughed and shook his head. "Just four flashes, a pause, then four more. All I want to know is that he's comin' down here."

Sharps's claw-like hand had disappeared somewhere with the money in it. His face had a handsome glow and his little eyes were watering.

He stood up smiling. "Sheriff, most of my friends is dead. It's lonely sometimes, thinkin' back. But a man gets used to most things. I got a good horse, with a little age on him but he's honest. And I got as honest a little jennet-mule as ever come down the pike. She'll even pack a bear, so you know she's a real sweetheart . . . Well, I think about you now'n then. We're friends."

Mark Hall stood up and pushed out a big paw of a hand. "Always will be," he said, and as the old man moved soundlessly to the door he also said, "Be careful up there, Eliza. I'll worry about you."

When the office was empty Sheriff Hall went to the stove for a cup of java but the stove was cold and the pot was empty so he stood facing the roadway with his back to the stove feeling a peculiar tightness in the chest for an old pot-hunter.

A Mexican *arriero* had once told him that when a man saw a very old person, he could believe that the old person had been very bad during his better years. God's punishment was worse than a bullet in the head. Far worse. He made them live so long that every*thing* they had cared for was changed, and every*one* they had cared for was dead. They lived on and on with bitter ashes for memories.

A dusty, faded man stepped into the doorway jerking Mark Hall's mind out of its solemn reverie. The man had folded riding-gloves under his shell-belt. He was smiling as he extended a calloused hand. "Morgan Trevithick, Sheriff Hall. I'm rangeboss for Mister van der Work who's got some land south of Bannonville a few miles."

The sheriff motioned toward a seat and went over to his desk to sit down. He was interested in the bronzed, work-hardened rangeboss. He was becoming interested in just about everything that had to do with van der Work. He offered his tobacco sack and papers but Trevithick was a chewer and dug out his plug as he said, "I come to town to hire a couple more riders. Two quit me couple of days ago." Trevithick paused until he had the cud tongued into his cheek. "We got a drive comin' from the east. Mister van der Work meant every word of it when he said he was goin' to liquidate his holdings down in Denver and put everythin' into land and cattle because that's where the most money would be in the years ahead."

Sheriff Hall rolled a cigarette, lit it and smiled at the darkly tanned man. "Maybe he's right. How many head are you running now?"

"Last count more'n two thousand cows. Add in one bull for every forty cows, and it makes a respectable number."

Mark Hall trickled smoke as he nodded his head. "Takes a heap of grass, Mister Trevithick."

The rangeboss flashed strong white teeth in a broad smile as he replied. "Yes sir, for a damned fact it does. Mister van der Work bought up the Silver place north of our other holdings, and that'll help."

Sheriff Hall blew smoke at the ceiling then punched out his cigarette. "Too bad about Charley Silver," he said quietly, and the rangeboss agreed.

"I didn't know him. Only come across him once on the range, but he seemed like a hell of a nice old feller."

"He was, Mister Trevithick."

"But someone didn't like him, Sheriff. Did you figure out who it was?"

"No I didn't. It's a pure mystery. That kind of a killin' is hard to figure out. No reason, no sign worth a damn. I've run across them before. They usually just sort of fade from memory."

Morgan Trevithick arose, shook Hall's hand again and turned from the door to say, "Just thought I'd ought to meet you, Sheriff. I'll be busy as hell for the next few weeks with those Texas cattle. But when I get a chance I'll ride up here again."

Hall arose and nodded. "Be lookin' forward to it, and good luck with the cattle."

After Trevithick had departed Hall sat

down and stared at his hands. Trevithick seemed to be strictly a cowman. Or he was one hell of a good actor and Hall had never known a rangeman who was a good actor.

He picked up his hat and left the office to make a routine round of the town.

6

Dust

THE saloonman met Sheriff Hall over in front of the harness works to tell him a couple of former riders of that gunsel down in Denver who was buying up land had been in his saloon. They told him who van der Work's foreman was, a man named Morgan Trevithick, which Sheriff Hall already knew but nodded his head anyway, and the saloonman told him something which formed the basis for some chilling thoughts he had later.

"They quit because more cattle was comin' all the time and Trevithick isn't hirin' more riders fast enough, which overworks everyone. The riders are putting in fifteen-hour days and unless Trevithick finds more men he's goin' to lose the ones he's got."

Sheriff Hall thanked the saloonman and finished his round of the town before returning to the office. Trevithick had said some Texas cattle were coming. He also said he thought they now had about a couple thousand head, and although he'd explained van der Work's plan, probably as it had been explained to him, he did not mention more cattle on their way other than the drive from Texas.

Hall rolled a smoke, got comfortable at his desk and started to envision a countryside overrun with cattle belonging to some wealthy man who, it seemed, was obsessed with an idea of creating a beef empire based upon many thousands of animals so that when the demand he anticipated came and prices went up, he could make millions.

Hall found no fault with van der Work's idea. There were many stockmen who expanded, sold expensive meat and got rich. They accomplished those things within the law and Mark Hall was becoming increasingly suspicious that this was not the way Mister van der Work meant to operate.

It also troubled him that there apparently was no limit to van der Work's ability to buy herds of cattle, but there definitely were limits to the cattle-carrying capacity of the countryside, and, none of the Bannonville cattle country was fenced.

Hall smashed his quirley. If van der Work was short-handed with more cattle arriving every few days, every week or so, regardless of how many hours Trevithick and his riders put in there would be a serious 'drift' problem.

In open range country there was always drift, especially in spring and summer when grass and water were so abundant cattle had no reason not to drift. But responsible ranchers used cowboys to check the drift as best they could.

If van der Work's thousands of cattle got to drifting out of control, the cowmen who lost grass to them would react as predictably as cattlemen had always reacted to that kind of thing and Mark

Hall would have a damned range war on his hands.

He was beginning to very seriously dislike a man he had never met.

When he felt sufficient time had elapsed for Eliza Sharps to be back in his highlands he walked to the extreme north end of town where a widow-woman lived who took in washing and did mending. Her little house was about twenty yards from the next structure southward. Northward she had an unobstructed view of open country all the way to the distant mountaintops.

He offered her two silver dollars if she would keep watch at her north window, and explained what she should watch for. She was pleased at the opportunity to earn money sitting down while not using her hands or arms.

Hall was heading back southward when in the bare places between buildings at the upper end of town he caught glimpses of rising dust.

For lack of anything else to hold his interest, and ready to believe the dust was being made by rangemen heading for town in a rush, which appeared at times to be the only way they ever rode, Sheriff Hall lost interest as he progressed southward until storefronts placed side by side cut off his westerly view.

Southward upon the opposite side of the road from the jailhouse three men were having difficulty with a horse tied to a hitchrack in front of the blacksmith's shop. Mark Hall watched for a few moments, unamused and solemn, while other onlookers, closer to the scene of dust, swearing and nimble scrambling, were hooting with delight and calling advice.

Hall turned in the jailhouse door to watch and when Ike Cameron came along the sheriff said, "That blacksmith's been here six years that I know of, and look at that. When a blindfold don't work, the horse keeps on fightin' and kickin' and tryin' to throw himself, you dump him, tie him and shoe him wrongside up."

The gunsmith sprayed tobacco juice before speaking. His voice sounded a little tired when he said, "Just because a man's been doin' something five or ten years only means he was taught to do it one way. Mister Hall, if he don't ever figure better ways, no one can tell him." Cameron raised his head, shifted his gaze southward beyond town and said, "Well now, what the hell is that?"

It was the source of that dust Hall had seen earlier: a battered old sturdy ranch wagon careening in from the west to take the turn that put it squarely in the centre of the stageroad. The team was lathered, the man with the lines was half-sitting, half-crouching with wind in his face as he kept the animals running. To one side two horsemen kept abreast.

The intuitive alarm lawmen developed if they remained with that line of work a number of years, was going full bore in the back of Mark Hall's head.

He pushed past the gunsmith, heading for the middle of the road. The man driving the belly-down horses yelled at the top of his lungs and gestured desperately for Hall to get out of his way.

Ike Cameron yelled from the plankwalk. "Sheriff! I don't think he can stop!"

Whether he could or not he clearly was not going to. Sheriff Hall moved clear as the rig swept past. One of the mounted men reined back, waited until some of the dust had settled, then rode on a sweaty horse toward the plankwalk and said, "It's Mister Talbot, Sheriff. He's been shot."

Hall's eyes became fixed on the red-faced, sweaty cowboy. "Dead?"

"Well, no. Leastways he wasn't when we wrapped him an' put him in the wagon. But the ride might have done it." The cowboy looked up where the rig had stopped in front of a small, unpainted residence. "I better get up there, Sheriff. Someone's got to walk them horses or they'll founder sure as hell."

When Sheriff Hall remained motionless watching the horseman walk away leading his spent animal, the gunsmith scowled. "Aren't you goin' up there?"

Hall turned just his head, eyed the older man for a moment and said something that did not make one lick of sense to Ike Cameron.

"Another one. Adjoining ranges. All Eliza's goin' to find up there is his empty camp."

The gunsmith stopped chewing to watch Mark Hall cross to the opposite plankwalk and start northward past gawking townspeople who had heard the noise, had hastened out of stores in time to see the ranch wagon nearly run down the sheriff, and were now gabbling like a herd of geese.

There were two men cooling out the winded horses. People on both sides of the road watched, spoke back and forth among themselves but made no move to approach the rangemen or the little unpretentious house where the third rangeman stood slouching in the doorway as though to keep people out.

He straightened up when Mark Hall appeared, was a little slow moving clear and got a rough shove as the sheriff shouldered past.

The rangeman came in behind Hall, red-faced and bristling. "They don't want no one in there," he said, reaching for the sheriff's sleeve.

Hall turned, shook the hand free and glared for a brief moment, then blew out a pent-up breath and spoke. "All right. Is the midwife in there with him?"

"Yes. Maybe we was lucky she was home."

"What happened?"

"Ain't sure. He was out with another feller lookin' for hung-up heifers. The other feller heard the shot but had a little time placing its direction, so he sashayed back and forth until he seen Ben's horse. Ben was lying in the grass on his face with blood all over hell. The rider raced back to the yard, we hitched a team to the wagon an' went back with blankets and the doctorin' box." The cowboy paused, glanced past at a closed door, then went on speaking. "Shot in the back. Not much of a hole in an' out but plenty of bleeding. We got him into the rig and raced for town."

Sheriff Hall looked steadily at the tall cowboy. "Who was out there with him?"

The tall man shook his head. "It wasn't him, Sheriff."

Hall waited for the flash of irritation to pass. "Who was with him? I didn't say he did the shooting, I want to know what he saw."

The tall man's eyes skittered away then back. "Well, he's the greying rider out front helpin' to cool out the horses. Jim Nettles."

Sheriff Hall's brows dropped quizzically. "What about him? What is it you're not saying?"

"Well, he's one of our men who said he seen a man on a black horse sittin' out a half-mile or so from the yard one time. Ben went out lookin' for sign of a rider an' there wasn't none."

Hall's dark scowl deepened. "What about it?"

"Well, he swore up an' down he seen that horseman again when we was headin' back to the yard with Ben in the wagon. He looked back and swore up an' down he seen that same feller in the distance sittin' out there watchin' us." The cowboy made a weak smile. "Jim's a good man. The best roper we got."

Hall nodded at the cowboy. "But he keeps a bottle hid out somewhere."

"Yeah."

Sheriff Hall considered the tall man for a moment before speaking again. "I'm going in there."

The cowboy gave a little shrug and Hall crossed to the closed door, entered a room darkened by blankets over two windows but well-enough lighted by three coal-oil lamps.

Ben Talbot was bare from the waist up, unconscious and making little fluttery sounds as he breathed. The grey-haired woman working over him raised testy eyes, recognised Sheriff Hall, looked down and went back to work.

Her name was Bertha Bradley. She was large-boned, heavy, wore her mane twisted into a knot at the nape of her neck and was as near to a doctor as Bannonville had. She was a midwife, but she also doctored illnesses, wounds, broken bones and injuries. She was also acknowledged as the best person around to treat fistulas, galls, bowed tendons and 'Monday-morning-sickness' in horses.

She ignored the sheriff's presence over by the door even when she eventually straightened back to wash her hands in one of several basins of water on a little table near the wooden platform where Talbot was lying. She looked at Talbot, her lips pulled flat, raised the back of one hand to push back a loose strand of grey hair, then went back to work still as though Sheriff Hall was not in the room.

He watched. He had seen her set broken bones among other things, but he had never before seen her work on a bullet wound.

She had large, work-roughened hands. They moved with confident deftness, never made a wasted motion, and seemed to have a touch as light as a feather.

When she straightened back the second time to rinse and dry her hands she finally spoke, but while still watching Ben Talbot, not Sheriff Hall.

"It's inside that worries me. I don't get any more serious bleeding when I squeeze the holes, but he could still be bleeding inside." She finished with the towel and put it aside. "If the bushwhacker had been closer, he would be dead." She finally faced Sheriff Hall. "He may be dying right now. The best I can say is that the bullet went clean through. The worst I can tell you, Mister Hall, is that if he's leakin' inside he may hang on for a while but in the end he'll die."

She looked back toward the wooden table. "He's a strong man. Not young, but healthy and tough." She leaned with her finger extended. "That's where it hit him. I'd have to roll him over to show you where it went out and broke a rib as it exited. From behind, Sheriff. I think from a fair distance, and according to my doctoring books, there is a fifty-fifty chance that because it was well over to one side, it didn't bust open any vital pieces of him. But that's what I can't be sure of and, like I said, if the bleeding inside is no worse now than the outside bleeding around those little holes, he'll make it. If not he won't."

The large woman used both hands this time to put that annoying straggle of hair back where it would stay, then went to a chair and sat down, still looking at Ben Talbot. "I was making bread in the kitchen. I'd just set it to rise near the stove." Her doughty gaze lifted to Hall's face. "In your line of work does it sometimes seem that some kind of downright ornery fate just waits until your hands are full to dump something like this in your lap?"

Sheriff Hall smiled. "Almost every day. Bertha? I want you to do something for me."

"If I can, Sheriff."

"You can. I'll go out and tell his men they can go back to the ranch. I'll tell them you'll keep Ben here and doctor him, an' that he seems to be doing well."

She nodded. "That's the truth, except for the 'doing well' part, and it may be true too, but right now I wouldn't bet a new hat on it."

Sheriff Hall let her finish. "That's the first part of what I want you to do. The second part is, I'll come back tonight after supper to see how he's comin' along. An' whether he's still with us or not, I'm going to spread word around town that the bullet knocked him off his horse and he bled like a stuck hog. That he's out of his head most of the time and even when he isn't what he says don't make any sense. An' he'll recover. He lost a lot of blood but he's strong enough to recover."

She was gazing at Sheriff Hall with a serene expression. When he had finished speaking she put her head slightly to one side in a sceptical way and smiled a little. "Do you think it will work, Sheriff?"

He smiled back. "I don't have any idea about that, but I know one thing about him — if it's who I think it is — he's as elusive as a ghost."

"Then he may not want to risk trying again, Sheriff."

He conceded that point. "He may not, but if he don't I have a feeling he's goin' to maybe lose his job. They usually get pretty well paid, Bertha." He stopped speaking, gazed at her for a long time, and decided to confide in her a little more, mainly because if there was another attempt to kill Ben Talbot, it might very well be made right here in her house. She should be warned.

"I'll know if he heads down this way. I'll be waitin' for him."

She let that pass because her female curiosity was aroused. "Who does he work for?"

Mark Hall chuckled and shook his head. "I'm superstitious, Bertha. It's always seemed to me that when I don't keep some things to myself, they turn out bad."

She arose to approach Ben Talbot and was looking at him when she spoke

88

softly. "I'm not a medical doctor. Sometimes that's frustrated the hell out of me. But I'm a woman who knows enough about patching folks up to do a fair job, and the part that doesn't know anything about doctoring is my female intuition. Right now it's telling me this one will recover and that the other one won't."

"What other one?"

She smiled sweetly at him. "I'll see you to the door, Sheriff."

7

The Discernible Design

AFTER Talbot's riders left town Sheriff Hall had a stream of curious townsfolk who knew Ben Talbot had been shot, but from that point on the versions ranged all the way from a self-inflicted injury while cleaning his sixgun, to being attacked by hideout redskins from a secret rancheria hidden deep in the mountains.

He listened, volunteered nothing, slapped people on the back admitting that their version had possibilities and got rid of them. When he was left alone he stood at the little steel-barred front window looking out and smiling. Nobody really wanted to know what had happened to Ben Talbot, they wanted an audience for some theory of their own. Sometimes people came awfully close to confirming Mark Hall's suspicion that there were more horse's arses in this world than there were horses.

Ike Cameron was different, perhaps because he was old, had seen it all at least once, had a delicate balance of his judgment of people which teetered between fools and not fools, and also because he was genuinely interested in what had happened out at the Lard Bucket ranch.

He had known Ben Talbot many years, since he'd been a button and his paw had been alive. But most interesting to Sheriff Hall was what Ike had to say on another subject.

"That van der Work outfit's got men riding for it you wouldn't want to turn your back on. Henry Fogle at the bank bought an old Kentucky rifle, pretty as a picture an' well preserved. He never fired one. Didn't even know how to load it. He offered to pay me to teach him those things after I had taken his rifle a long way out and test-fired a few rounds through it." Ike squinted. "You got any idea of the range of those old rifled barrels, Sheriff?"

Hall shook his head.

"Accurate pretty close to a mile and still able to kill you at dang near twice that distance."

Sheriff Hall looked down his nose at the older man. Ike understood the look and said, "I'm telling you the gospel truth. Old and out-dated as those guns are, they can shoot rings around your factory-made Winchesters and Remingtons . . . Well, I hired a horse and rode about three, four miles in a southwesterly direction. Wanted to be plenty far so's the slugs wouldn't knock some poor damned fool off his wagon I couldn't even see." Ike went silent for a long time. When Mark Hall was about to prime him, the gunsmith started up again.

"For the best firin' of those long-barrelled pieces a man should use a rest. There's a tumble of big rocks out there. I'd used them before. I tied the horse back where the noise wouldn't make him set back, bust the shank and leave me afoot out there, then I got into the rocks, took my time about loadin' and all, selected a target I could barely see and fired off a round, set back to swab out and re-charge an' was squintin' out yonder to see if I'd hit the target, which I never did know, when a sweaty, unwashed lookin' man who hadn't shaved in a week came up over the rocks behind me with a cocked Colt in his fist. He asked me what in the hell I thought I was doing. I told him — sightin' in that old gun for a feller in town."

Ike lapsed into another of those lengthy silences but did not come out of it this time until Sheriff Hall said, "Go on. I'm listening."

"Well, there was three of them. They'd snuck up south of me slicker'n grease. Sheriff, I know I'm gettin' along, but my eyesight is as good as it ever was. I didn't see — "

"How about your hearing?" Hall interrupted to drily ask.

Cameron looked up, then away. "All

right, I didn't hear them, but I should have seen them. Unless they was professional skulkers. Then most likely I wouldn't have because I wasn't expecting anything like that."

"What did they say?"

"That they worked for van der Work, that I was on his land, that he didn't like trespassers and I'd better shag my butt out of there. Which I did."

"Ever see any of them before, Ike?"

"Not that I recollect," the gunsmith replied thoughtfully while watching a dung-beetle wrestling with something a horse had left near the jailhouse hitchrack. "And I got to tell you, Sheriff, I'd have to look on it as a real kindness of the Almighty if I never saw 'em again." He looked up, straight at Sheriff Hall, and asked a question: "Those rocks are big an' sort of crumbly with red streaks. You know the ones I'm talkin' about?"

The sheriffs brow furrowed as he said, "I think so. Are there In'ian scratchings on them?"

"Yep. You know them," stated

94

Cameron, continuing to gaze at the lawman. "They are at least a mile inside the boundary of Ben Talbot's ranch. He showed 'em to me years ago and also showed me how far south of them his property line was."

Hall leaned on the hitchrack to also consider the persistent but not very intelligent way the dung-beetle was going about rolling his prize toward the edge of the roadway. This time it was the gunsmith who had to get things going again.

"On the ride back to town I got thinkin' about this van der Work individual. He got the Mason and Arledge places, and there's talk around town that he's moved over to old Charley Silver's place, which adjoins his other holdings . . . Sheriff, you listening?"

Hall nodded without speaking nor taking his eyes off the extremely busy beetle.

"Well," stated Ike Cameron, "Arledge an' Mason adjoined Charley Silver, an' Charley's range adjoins Ben Talbot's

Lard Bucket range . . . And some son of a bitch shot Charley in the back, and some son of a bitch did the same to Ben Talbot . . . And I ran into three mean-lookin' sons of bitches I can tell you from bein' around human beings for one hell of a long time would do somethin' like that . . . What do you think?"

Sheriff Hall pushed up off the rack to watch a couple of local cowmen ride past. When they nodded he nodded back before answering his old friend. "Nothing I'd care to talk about right now, Ike. But I'm obliged for our talk. Come on over to the saloon and I'll stand us a round."

But the gunsmith was annoyed. "No thanks. Another time maybe. You know damned well I never repeat things."

Hall smiled. "I know that, Ike. But there's more to this mess than folks know and right now I'd as soon it stayed that way . . . Now wait a minute, I didn't mean I thought you'd go around shootin' off your mouth . . . "

But Ike Cameron was already striding angrily toward the opposite plankwalk.

Sheriff Hall squinted at the sun. The day was better than half spent, and if it was a fact that a man was a fool for at least five minutes of every day, and the trick was not to exceed his limit, he had just used up his five minutes, so he had to try like hell not to compound it for the five or six hours which were left before evening arrived.

He was leaving the general store after purchasing a fresh sack of Bull Durham when four riders entering town from the north end held his attention. The foremost among them was a very large man whose paunch had pushed his britches down to half-mast. He wore a white shirt, a rarity in cow country. He was also wearing a light coat that seemed to have no wrinkles and his new boots had six or eight rows of stitching on their uppers, all of it in multi-coloured thread.

The man's horse was as handsome a put-up chestnut as Mark Hall had ever seen. It was wearing a saddle and bridle with enough hand-engraved sterling silver to maybe pay off half the mortgages around town.

He was also armed. Not with a saddlegun but with a darkly blued sixgun with a yellowish bone handle.

The men riding with him, back a few feet, were typical of their calling; hard-riding, calloused, faded and weathered rangemen. They looked back when people on the sidewalks looked out at them.

Sheriff Hall leaned on an overhang upright to roll a smoke and watch as the big man turned in at the nearest tie-rack, which happened to be in front of Ike Cameron's shop, tied up and walked back to the midwife's little weathered house with one of his riders. The other two slouched in horse-shade at the tie-rack.

Sheriff Hall lit up, removed the quirley from his lips and went northward as far as the narrow dog-trot between the general store and the building next to it. He emerged in the back-alley and startled a rat-tailed mongrel dog who had been happily rooting in what had tumbled out of a trash barrel he had knocked over. He paused to drop the cigarette and stamp on it as the dog fled across the alley and left some hair on a hole in someone's wooden fence over there.

It required very little time for Sheriff Hall to reach the rear of the midwife's residence and although he was totally exposed to view from back there, he got as close to the door as possible and leaned down to listen.

The only distinguishable sound was made by knotty wood popping in a cook-stove. Evidently Bertha Bradley's alley-door opened out of her kitchen.

He tried the knob. The door yielded inward but it also grated on its spindles so Sheriff Hall exerted upward pressure to force the hinges tight, and stepped inside, left the door open and glanced at the popping stove. The aroma from a pot-roast was all-pervasive. He took four long steps to reach the next door, which was closed, and put his ear against it. This time he distinctly heard a deep, authoritative voice speaking curtly. " . . . Glad he'll make it. I won't be able to come back in three days, but you can tell him Mister van der Work was here and that I'd like to talk to him."

Bertha's voice was calm as she replied to the large man. "I'll tell him and I'm sorry I can't let anyone see him right now. He needs all the rest he can get. You'll understand."

Van der Work replied in the same brusque manner. "Yes. I understand. And I am sure that in your care he'll do very well. By the way, does anyone around Bannonville know what happened to him? Does anyone know who might have shot him? By any chance did he see the bushwhacker? Has he mentioned anything to you about the shooting?"

"No, Mister van der Work. He comes and goes. Talks gibberish and loses consciousness. As far as I've heard, the shooting is a mystery."

"The sheriff, Mrs Bradley . . . ?"

"I don't know. He was here the day

they brought him but I haven't seen him since."

"Well; it was pleasant meeting you, Mrs Bradley. As I said, I hope Talbot makes it. Good day."

Sheriff Hall heard them walking toward the roadway door out of the parlour and went over to a kitchen table, sat down, placed his hat on the floor and leaned back taking down deep inhalations of kitchen fragrance.

When Bertha Bradley walked in with knitted brows and a pursed mouth, she gave a slight start and went toward a chair with a hand over her heart.

"I suppose you eavesdropped," she told him, and when Hall nodded she also paused, then glared. "You almost gave me heart failure. He was bad enough, little pale eyes never blinking and that half-smiling, unwashed rider of his standing back there leering. And you sneaking into my kitchen like a burglar." She arose and went briskly to open the oven and pull out the roast in its nest of potatoes, carrots and onions.

The fragrance was almost overpowering. Sheriff Hall moved over to look past her shoulder as he said, "How did he know Ben was here?"

"He didn't say and I didn't ask. What's the matter with you, Sheriff? Haven't you eaten lately?"

"Not anything like that, Bertha. I haven't even smelled anything like that for so long I can't remember."

She hoisted the hot pan to the stove-top, placed its covering slightly to one side so the meat would cool gradually, and looked straight at Mark Hall. "Mister Talbot ought to like that, don't you think?"

Sheriff Hall nodded. "Yes indeed. It's a pity a man has to be shot to get fed like that."

"He doesn't have to," the large woman said, and pointed toward the table. "Sit down. No, go out back and wash up first." She cocked her head at him. "Why don't you get married, Sheriff? Cafe-food will ruin your insides if you don't eat anything else."

Hall was in the doorway when he looked back at her. "You're temptin' the hell out of me, Bertha. I had no idea you could cook like this. I'll think about it."

As he disappeared from sight the large woman's face got red as a beet and she stamped out of the kitchen to look in on Ben Talbot.

He was not only sleeping, he was snoring. She used a cool rag from a basin of water to gently wipe sweat off his face. He did not move. The cadence of his snoring did not change even when she leaned to very gently pull each of his bandages far enough so that she could see the swollen, purplish wounds.

When she returned to the kitchen Sheriff Hall was gone. Even his hat was gone. She stood a long moment trying to decide whether to set the table for two or not, decided not to and went to work making up a supper platter for her patient.

The reason Mark Hall was no longer there was because when he'd returned from washing, and had not found her in the kitchen, he'd walked on through to the parlour and stood at a roadside window looking southward.

That magnificent chestnut horse wearing the silver-mounted outfit was dozing at the tie-rack in front of his jailhouse. It was the only animal down there so Mister van der Work had probably yielded to the importunities of his rangeriders to visit the local waterhole.

Sheriff Hall hastened across the road and southward toward his office. He had pretty much already made up his mind about Henry van der Work, and while he did not expect a face-to-face meeting to change that very much, he was curious about the man stopping by his office.

8

The Big Man

VAN DER WORK was comfortable in a chair, relaxed, thick legs pushed out, smoking a fragrant cigar. When the sheriff apologised for not being around, the big, fleshy man made a casual wave with the cigar. "People should be busy, Sheriff. All my life I've mistrusted folks who aren't."

Hall went to fire up the stove. The fleshy man watched indifferently and when the sheriff went back to sit down at his desk van der Work said, "I just looked in on Ben Talbot. We'd never met, and I heard about the shooting."

Mark Hall nodded, wearing no expression. "How was he?"

"That woman who's taking care of him said he couldn't have visitors for about another three days. Otherwise, I

105

got the impression that he's on the mend." Van der Work removed the cigar and regarded Sheriff Hall. "You haven't been up to see him since he was shot?"

Sheriff Hall shook his head. "No. The lady up there told me he's unconscious a good bit of the time an' when he isn't he mumbles things that don't make sense. I'll wait until he's able to sit up and talk sense." Hall leaned back. "But I doubt he'll be able to be much help. He was riding with one of his men when he got shot, an' the other man don't know anything either."

"Did he have enemies, Sheriff?"

Hall smiled. "Everyone has enemies, Mister van der Work."

The fleshy man nodded as he plugged the fragrant cigar back between his teeth. He looked around the room as he spoke again. "Did you meet an old feller named Albert George a few weeks back?"

Sheriff Hall considered the coarse, jowly profile of the large man. "Yes, I met him. We had a long talk in fact.

I had no idea you had got hold of the Silver ranch."

Van der Work's heavy features turned back to Sheriff Hall slowly, his little blue eyes stone-blank. "I've used him several times down in the city to make title searches and the like for me. He didn't get back to Denver alive. A stage he and three other people were passengers on went over the edge of a precipice. The drop was about six hundred feet. Horses, coach and all. They seem to think a rattlesnake was sunning in the road when the stage came along, scairt the leaders and they shied sideways — right over the edge."

Mark Hall was shocked. He would not miss Albert George but that seemed to be a hell of a way to die — falling six hundred feet knowing what would happen every foot of the way. "I'm sorry," he said, and the large, fleshy man inclined his head slowly, as though he'd expected some statement like that. "I've got another man to do what Albert George did. His name is Henderson. He

TFH8

may want to meet you, Sheriff."

Van der Work pushed upwards out of the chair. When he was standing erect he was an impressive figure of a man, large, portly, commanding, exuding success, and likely to inspire respect.

Mark Hall also arose. They were about the same height and while Hall was a heavy man, he was not fat and van der Work was.

The paunchy man removed the cigar and while gazing at its lighted tip, he said, "Out here, Sheriff, the future will belong to the man with the most cattle."

Hall's comment was drily made. "The country will only carry so many head, Mister van der Work. It's already got some big herds on some pretty big ranches."

Van der Work bit down on the cigar as he eyed Sheriff Hall. "If this whole basin belonged to one man, Sheriff, and Bannonville depended on his trade to survive, would you feel right about protecting his interests to keep your job and to keep your town alive?"

Hall returned the other man's gaze without blinking. "It'd be something to think about, Mister van der Work."

The large man solemnly inclined his head and turned to depart. Sheriff Hall watched him go, sat down, considered his scarred large hands atop the desk, and let go with a long sigh.

The possum-bellied son of a bitch was as secretive about his plans as a foghorn, and about as subtle as a ton of rock. He was out to own the entire countryside, and so far he'd bought out two ranchers, had acquired another ranch in a way that troubled Mark Hall, and had evidently made no secret about eventually owning Talbot's Lard Bucket ranch, or else old Ike hadn't heard those hard cases right he had encountered out yonder at the crumbly rocks.

As though materialising out of the sheriff's thoughts, Ike appeared in the doorway. When their eyes met he said, "Did you see those fellers who was with that big man on the silver saddle? Those are the men I told you about; the ones who snuck up on me out yonder at the crumbly rocks."

Hall went to stoke up the little iron stove and put the coffee-pot atop it. He said nothing until he'd returned to his chair. "The other one was the feller who got the Silver place. Van der Work."

Cameron sat down. "Did you know they come into town from the north?"

"Yes."

"Well now," stated the gunsmith, "don't all the range he owns lie south of town? Then what d'you suppose he was doin' up northward, unless maybe he'd been ridin' over Ben Talbot's land, maybe to get an idea of what he might get if Ben dies?"

Sheriff Hall offered a wintery little smile. "You're a sly old buzzard, Ike. To be right frank with you, I kind of like the idea of him bein' up here."

Cameron's brows dropped, suspicion showed in his stare. "He didn't buy you, Mark."

Sheriff Hall chuckled. "He didn't offer

to, but he told me some things worth thinking about."

Cameron continued to regard Sheriff Hall for a long time before he arose and turned toward the door. "Secrets again," he muttered, and stamped out into the roadway, indignant all over again.

Sheriff Hall had to drink coffee alone.

Later, along toward late afternoon, he went up to the saloon for the barman's judgment of van der Work's hired men. It wasn't condemnatory although the saloonman did mention an impression that they were hard men, and if van der Work had a few more like that, and someone started trouble with him, they damned well might find themselves hock-deep in it.

Hall went along to the cafe for an early supper, then returned to Bertha Bradley's house north of the gunshop and opposite Hank McHenry's saddle and harness works. Hank, who was a greying, grizzled, hawk-faced man who stood and walked with a slight stoop, was drinking coffee with Ike Cameron when

111

Sheriff Hall passed by. He put aside his cup, arose, reached the doorway in two long steps and called.

"Sheriff! You got a minute?"

Hall turned back. They did not enter the gunshop but where Cameron was sitting he could hear everything they said without trying to. The stork-like harness-maker jutted a stubbly jaw in the direction of his business establishment across the road. "Two of them riders that work for that rich fat man was left at the tie-rack when he went up to Bertha's place, got tired of just waitin' I guess, an come over to my place. One of 'em left a torn spur strap, said he'd be back for it in a few days, and got to talkin' about Bannonville."

"What was his name?"

"Damned if I know."

From back in the gloom Ike Cameron sang out. "That's the one that came up out of the rocks behind me with a cocked gun in his hand, Sheriff."

Hall looked through the gloom where Ike was sitting, then returned his attention to the harness-maker. "What about Bannonville, Hank?"

"Just a lot of questions, sort of general talk right up until he told me his employer might someday buy up the town. An' until he got around to doin' that, he'd be acquirin' land and cattle. An' that he'd get rid of the local cattle because he aims to have only bred-up redbacks, an' mostly what he's seen in the country so far is Texas-cross cattle."

Cameron came to lean in the door. He looked bleakly at Mark Hall when the sheriff said, "Sounds like a windbag to me, Hank."

Cameron snorted. "I never noticed it before Sheriff, but I'm beginnin' to wonder if you aren't one of those folks who can't see a tree for the forest."

Hall faced his old friend. "What does that mean, Ike?"

"It means you got trouble comin' straight at you, an' you can't see it. Come on, Hank, we ain't finished the coffee."

After the older men retreated back

into the gloom of the gunshop Sheriff Hall resumed his walk in the direction of Bertha Bradley's house. Of course he knew trouble was coming. And he knew about how it was going to arrive — on a black horse — but he would not explain what he knew and what he suspected even to townsmen he knew could be trusted like Cameron and McHenry, because he really was superstitious about revealing things.

Bertha met him at the door, moved aside for him to enter and apologised for the mediciny smell of her house. She had been cleaning out Ben Talbot's wounds. For that purpose she used carbolic acid, and later, a special concoction she made of lanolin, herbs and rose-oil.

Sheriff Hall wasn't sure the place didn't smell like one of those big saloons in cities where a man could get a woman to dance with him for two-bits, but he wouldn't have said anything like that to save his soul.

She stopped in the centre of the parlour with her head slightly on one side and asked why he had disappeared after she'd invited him to supper. He told her of seeing van der Work's horse down in front of the jailhouse, and a little about his meeting with the big, fleshy man. For her part, Bertha said it was not too late for supper, and when he would have smiled in anticipation about that, she made another remark.

"Mister Talbot's much better. He ate like a wolf but mostly, he drank water. He wants to sit up but I can't have him bleeding again so he's lying flat out."

"He's rational?"

"As you are, Sheriff. Would you like to see him?"

Bertha led the way. Talbot's room was evidently an after thought; the ceiling sloped toward the back wall where it was so low a person had to crouch down, but nearer the front wall where the doorway was, it was higher. There was a blanket nailed over the only window in the room, which faced the alley, and the room smelled of coal-oil from two lamps atop a chifferobe against the south wall.

Ben Talbot had a thin, measly pillow under his head. He needed a shave badly, but his eyes were clear when he met Mark Hall's questioning look, and he smiled as Bertha leaned over to adjust the tan army blanket that covered him. He said, "I got a notion to marry her, Mark. What do you think?"

Hall was so relieved he smiled. "I think you could do a lot worse, Ben. A whole lot worse."

Bertha acted as though nothing had been said as she moved toward the doorway. "When you're finished, Sheriff, supper will be waiting."

Ben Talbot followed the large woman's retreating figure before saying, "Has she taken a shine to you, Mark?"

"Yeah. The same shine she'd take to a hungry dog . . . Ben?"

"I know what you are goin' to ask and I'll tell you straight out I didn't see him. I was heading for a patch of thick, tall chaparral. There's a sump-spring through it a dozen or so yards. Years past we've missed findin' cattle

116

in there. Lots of times. You can't see through the brush and if they're not moving or making noise you don't know they are in there."

"But he was," said the sheriff drily.

"Must have been," Talbot conceded and raised his eyes. "But he made it a long shot, so they told me, an' I keep askin' myself why he didn't wait until I was closer to the thicket, or maybe workin' my way through it?"

Sheriff Hall made a sardonic judgment about that. "He's a hired killer, Ben. A professional. Like all professionals my guess is that it was a matter of professional pride that he could knock you off your horse at a distance. He's got an ivory front-sight on his carbine."

The flat-out wounded man looked unwaveringly at Mark Hall. "You know who he is?"

"I got some ideas about him, but I don't know his name or anything personal about him." When Hall finished answering Talbot's question he swung a chair around, straddled it, with his hands

117

on the high back to lean his chin on. "Ben, do you recollect ever meetin' a big, paunchy man who rides a lot of silver whose name is van der Work?"

Talbot's response was short. "Never met him but I heard it was him bought the Charley Silver place. He already owned the Mason and Arledge places."

Hall continued to lean broodingly on the chair back.

"Somethin' has bothered me since you came to town to tell me about Charley. You said he'd maybe been dead a couple of days. You also said you went back to bury him in another few days an' the wagon was still there. Ben; did you turn his team horses loose; were they still standing there three, four days later when you went out to plant Charley?"

Talbot's brows puckered in a frown. "Well hell no," he replied. "The horses wasn't on the rig after my riders found Charley dead down there. They took the horses off the tongue, dumped the harness in the grass an' turned the horses loose. I thought you knew that."

Hall hadn't known it, and it had bothered him but it had been cleared up very naturally and normally, and he was willing to abandon the subject so he asked another question. "You're sure you didn't see anything about the time you got shot?"

"Dead sure."

"Well, that rider you had with you saw something, Ben. He saw a feller on a black horse sitting far out lookin' back."

Talbot weakly raised a hand to disgustedly gesture with it. "Mark, he was the same man who said he'd seen this phantom horseman before, an' I told you, he drinks."

Hall nodded at his friend. "Yeah. Well, your cowboy didn't try to kill you, Ben, but someone sure as hell did, didn't they?"

Talbot's expression showed bafflement, but it also showed a hint of exasperation. "Yeah, someone tried to kill me, but it wasn't any ghost-rider. That's gettin' to be a legend, Mark, and it's plain old bull."

Sheriff Hall arose to depart. "I saw him," he said, and went out to be fed Bertha's potroast, leaving Ben Talbot staring at the empty doorway.

9

The Fast Gun

DAWN came a little earlier every month after February. By full summer, sunlight awakened late-sleepers several hours before breakfast, if their windows happened to face the east as the sheriff's window did.

He'd had all the sleep he needed anyway. By the time he was ready to cross over and hike down to the cafe for breakfast there was a flattening, high skiff of fragrant woodsmoke settling over Bannonville where householders were getting ready for the new day.

A few other early diners were already arrayed along the counter. Behind them the window was obscured by steam. The cafe smelled of frying meat and black coffee when Sheriff Hall settled between the local blacksmith and Hank McHenry

121

the harness-maker. They nodded. Hall nodded back. No one offered to strike up a conversation. The cafeman's establishment had about a dozen unsmiling individuals waiting to be fed who hunched across the counter eyeing the pie table, not exactly surly but not congenial either, waiting for that first cup of java of the day.

A young boy came rushing in, let the door slam, ignored the baleful glares he got for that and tugged at the sheriff's sleeve. He would not speak but he was very insistent otherwise so Hall followed him outside. There, the boy pointed a skinny arm northward and said, "Widder-woman who lives in that tarpaper shack above town give me five cents to find you and tell you to get up there right away."

By the time Sheriff Hall had stopped looking toward the north end of town the boy had vanished.

Hall forgot about breakfast. He hadn't forgotten about the woman north of town, but he'd almost decided old Eliza was not going to signal, or the woman had slept when she was supposed to be watching.

He hiked briskly through the morning chill and was met by the woman at her doorway. She closed the door behind him like a genuine conspirator and pointed to the window where she'd kept vigil. "The flashes came about a half-hour ago, Sheriff, four in a row, then nothing for a while, and four more flashes. Is that what you been waiting for?"

Hall nodded while digging in a trouser pocket. He handed her another silver dollar, thanked her and walked back toward the centre of town. At the jailhouse he fired up the stove and set the coffee-pot atop it. Over at the cafe customers entered and departed, the window was still opaque with steam, and Sheriff Hall rolled and lit a smoke as a substitute for his missed meal.

Because Sheriff Hall had never been all the way to the topout-country where Eliza Sharps did his best pot-hunting, he had to guess how long it would take the old man to reach town.

His guess was not until late tonight or tomorrow, and that held true for the bushwhacker who rode the black horse.

It was enough time for the sheriff to be prepared. He finally returned to the cafe by which time the counter was vacant except for one old gaffer noisily supping coffee who was sitting hunched while holding the cup in both hands and staring at nothing, or possibly staring down the shadowy tunnel of memory, but whatever it was he sat in a world of his own, oblivious to the sheriff and even the cafeman who came along to ask Hall how Mister Talbot was getting along and to casually volunteer something that brought Hall straight up on his seat.

"Last I heard," stated the sheriff, "he was on the mend."

The cafeman nodded about that. "Glad to hear it. Folks are sayin' that someone had ought to do somethin' about it. Two back-shootings in a row and no one's been brought in."

Mark Hall stopped eating to look at the cafeman.

He should have known, should have realised that people would be talking about something like this. Given enough time they would invariably arrive at a fairly general consensus, which was simply that the sheriff was not doing his job.

The cafeman avoided a meeting of eyes by swabbing his countertop and working particularly hard on a spot only he could see.

When Sheriff Hall was standing up counting out coins he said, "Human beings have a blind spot. Did you know that? One of the first things I learned when I was old enough to shave was never to pass judgment until I knew both sides."

He walked out of the cafe; the old gaffer had not moved, had scarcely blinked, but the cafeman was dropping the coins into his cash drawer while staring at the back of the big lawman crossing the road. As he shuffled back behind the blanket that curtained off his cooking area he wagged his head.

At the jailhouse Sheriff Hall had all the time in the world to take a Winchester from the wall rack, clean it, very lightly oil it, work the levering mechanism several times, then to load it, shove it into a scabbard which he leaned beside the front door, and sit down to put his sixgun atop the table for the same careful treatment, after he'd had a smoke.

It was during this moment of leisure that someone across the road and southward began working a cherry-red length of shoeing steel across an anvil. The strikes were perfectly spaced and solid. The sound carried all over town.

Hall loosened, trickled smoke and smiled at the far wall. He was fond of a number of things; the sound of steel being worked, the smell of a sweaty horse, sunrises more than sunsets, and the town that was murmuring behind his back.

He stubbed out the quirley, leaned

forward with an oily rag and went to work on the handgun. He thought about old Eliza. Years back someone had told him Eliza's real name was Elijah, but since he could neither read nor write, and because an army paymaster either did not or could not, make the distinction, and possibly too because he might have known someone named Eliza, maybe a woman, and could therefore readily spell the name, Elijah Sharps had become Eliza Sharps.

To the old pot-hunter the difference must have been simply one of pronunciation, and that was slight enough to pass scarcely noticed. Especially so if his hearing, like that of Ike Cameron, was good enough to pick up sounds, but not good enough to catch nuances.

Hall finished with the sixgun, went out back to wash oil off his hands, and remained out there watching someone down at the south end of town filling an old wagon with manure from a pile taller than he was which the liveryman had been adding to for weeks. He thought he knew who that was but the distance was too great so he went back inside. He knew everyone around the countryside who did not drift in with spring and drift out with autumn.

He went over to the general store, listened to gossip for a while, went up to the saloon to further take the pulse of his town, but the saloonman was discreet. He undoubtedly had heard the mutterings against Sheriff Hall, but if there was one verity in the life of saloonmen, it was not to repeat things. All he said, was: "I thought that big man with the silver riggin' left town yesterday."

Hall's eyes got round. "Didn't he?"

"Well, maybe he has by now, but that bullyin' loudmouth who rides for him was in here about a half-hour ago. The only time I've seen one, the other ain't far off."

Sheriff Hall returned to the roadway. Among the pedestrians, mostly women aiming for the general store with net shopping-bags, there was a sprinkling of men. Hall knew most of them. The ones he did not know held his attention until he was fairly satisfied they were not van der Work riders.

He was about ready to put the entire matter out of his mind when something that sounded like either a shouting-match or a fight erupted down at the billiard palace, also known as the pool-room. But by the time he got there whatever had caused the ruckus had ended. The pool-room proprietor stared at Sheriff Hall in his doorway with a surly look and two tousle-headed, tall youths were playing pool as though there had been no flare-up between them and the man who ran the place.

Hall returned to the roadway.

Tied at the rack in front of the harness works was a dozing, hip-shot horse. Hall abruptly remembered a torn spur strap and went up there. The moment he blocked out sunlight in the doorway he knew Hank McHenry was in a bad mood. He did not even glance up from his cutting-table where a full hide had been pegged out and moistened slightly.

Leaning on the counter was a stocky rangeman who had not shaved lately, and whose expression when he looked around toward the doorway, was half-smiling, half-challenging.

Hall walked in, nodded at the rider, considered McHenry and said, "Good morning, Hank."

The tall, slightly stooped older man raised sulphurous eyes. "Naw it ain't," he growled, and went back to work on damp leather.

Sheriff Hall watched him select a tin template from several hanging from nails on the wall, return to the table and place the pattern first in one place, then another. It was the template for a semisquare skirt. The obvious objective was to place it where the least trimming would be required in order to have more hide for the following patterns.

The husky, raffish cowboy said, "Up near the neck," and McHenry straightened up glaring. Whether he was going to speak or not, he did not get the chance. The cowboy leaned to gesture with his left hand. "Put the front up on the neck." He was smiling again. "That way the wrinkled leather'll be under the tree where no one'll see it."

He turned toward the sheriff. "Ain't that right?"

Hall leaned down on the counter eyeing the rangeman. "How many saddles have you made?" he asked.

The stocky man's smile faded slowly.

"You don't have to make saddles to know what makes sense and what don't, Sheriff."

Hall continued to regard the man. He had heard from Ike Cameron that the man was a bully. He had also guessed since entering the harness shop, that he had been badgering Hank.

Hall asked a question. "Did you get what you came in here for?"

The cowboy held up a patched spur leather. "Yeah. Look at that. I've seen blind little old ladies who could sew better'n that."

Hank was getting red in the face on the opposite side of the counter.

131

Sheriff Hall ignored the strap the man was holding up to him. "You got it. If you could have done any better you should have patched it yourself. Get on your horse and leave town."

McHenry finally spoke. "Wait a minute. He didn't pay. Said he wouldn't pay for that kind of a job."

Sheriff Hall's gaze was fixed on the husky rangeman. "Put the money on the counter."

The cowboy was wearing that half-smiling, half-truculent expression again, and as he replied to Mark Hall he straightened back gently from the counter. "An' if I don't?" he asked.

The sheriff had not moved. He was still leaning on the counter, his left arm partially against the counter, partially in front. "Then I'll lock you up until you do," he said quietly.

McHenry's checked-up anger had began to cool the moment instinct told him trouble was coming. "Sheriff," he said, "forget it. It's not worth gettin' up a sweat about. Hell, it's only two bits."

Hall did not once look away from the rangeman as he repeated his earlier statement: "Put the money on the counter."

Hank McHenry's face was losing colour. He was crowding seventy and most of those years had been spent on the frontier. He knew when an argument had gotten to the point where the arguers had only two choices, fight or saddle up, ride out, and spend the rest of their lives loathing themselves.

He also knew better than to move or make a sound.

The cowboy's overbearing smile was pegged into place but his eyes did not smile at all. "I guess you'll have to lock me up," he said, and pulled down a slow, deep breath.

Sheriff Hall waited. The cowboy had to let his breath out very slowly. As he was taking in one more deep-down breath Sheriff Hall cautioned him. "You'll never make it, whatever your name is who rides for van der Work."

That was the deliberate diversion. The

cowboy's eyes flickered in surprise at hearing a man he did not know make personal, truthful remarks about him.

Sheriff Hall's right hand blurred in a downward swoop and a rising swing. The rangeman had lost two seconds. Still, his gun cleared leather before the deafening muzzleblast made Hank McHenry recoil as though he'd been struck.

It was heard all over town too, but while people rushed to doorways and windows to scan the roadway, no one walked out into plain sight.

The cowboy struck Hank's little woodstove, knocked it loose of the pipe, which resulted in oily black soot flying in all directions.

The man's weapon skittered sideways, struck the base of the counter and stopped moving. Its owner flopped twice after landing against the little stove, rolled up onto his right side with an outflung arm under his head, and did not move again.

Hank ignored the settling oily soot, which he would never completely get rid of, and went to lean across the counter looking down as Sheriff Hall shucked out a spent casing and plugged in a fresh load from his belt. McHenry said, "Deader'n a damned stone." He straightened up a little. "For two damned bits. Got himself killed for a damned lousy quarter of a dollar."

Sheriff Hall was leathering his reloaded weapon when he disagreed with that. "Naw. It never was the two bits, Hank. He was damned fast. Even with a little handicap he got his gun out faster than I did, but I started sooner. Hank, somewhere, maybe in a lot of places, if folks knew he just got himself killed, they'd have a celebration. He was a bully at his best and only the Lord knows what he was at his worst, but I can guess."

10

Toward A Harrowing Night

ANY killing had a sobering, dampening effect on a town, but because this one was completely unexpected, added to the fact that there had not been another killing in Bannonville for eight years, resulted in a funereal mood that lingered long after the shock had passed.

Sheriff Hall had everything from the dead man's pockets in the victim's hat when he went down to his office to toss the dead man's gun on the desk. No one bothered him but up at McHenry's harness shop people not only arrived full of questions, but they tracked soot in and out until Hank's exasperation moved him to run them off, all but the gunsmith who helped clean up the place, and Cameron did not say ten words until they retreated to the back room where Hank lived, and sat down with dirty hands to share a bottle. Then, when McHenry recalled what had happened, Ike said, "Good riddance. That man was hit over the head with a mean stick the day he was born."

McHenry was still having trouble with the reason for the killing. He looked straight at Cameron as he said, "How many killings have you seen, Ike? Hell, I've seen men killed for gettin' drunk and thinkin' they was bulletproof, for stealin' someone's horse, for tryin' to stop trains, stagecoaches, an' for ridin' into ambushes. But I'll be damned if I ever saw one killed for two bits before."

Cameron's opinion of the dead man was unalterable. "Two bits or a thousand dollars, it's still good riddance. What'd Mark say afterwards?"

"Nothing. Not a word. He cleaned out the feller's pockets, took his gun, and walked out of here."

"Who hauled the carcass away?"

"Three men. Two from the blacksmith's

shed an' a big Messican from the corralyard. Maybe Mark sent 'em, I didn't ask an' they didn't tell me." McHenry refilled their little glasses and downed his without waiting for his friend to reach for his glass. "Two lousy damned bits. One quarter of a dollar."

Out front someone was hammering on the roadway door. McHenry ignored it. The hammering continued at intervals for close to five minutes then stopped.

The man who had been out there went down to the jailhouse where Sheriff Hall was sorting through the dead man's effects. When he walked in and their eyes met, Hall said, "Have a chair, Mister Trevithick," and scooped the articles on his desktop into the same old greasy hat he had brought them down there in, and leaned with clasped hands gazing at van der Work's rangeboss.

Trevithick tipped his hat back before speaking. "What happened?"

"He had the harness-maker patch a spur leather then wouldn't pay him. When I told him to put the money on the counter he got set to fight."

The rangeboss studied the scuffed toes of his boots for a while before speaking again. "I didn't know him very well. Mister van der Work brought him up here with two other men. They didn't mix much with the other riders. When the boss rode out they went with him."

Sheriff Hall said, "Where are the other two?"

Trevithick didn't know. "I've been too busy to keep track, Sheriff."

"Where is Mister van der Work?"

Trevithick frowned at the toes of his boots again. "Well; he said he was goin' to ride up north, look over the country." The rangeboss's eyes swept upwards. "My guess is that the other two are with him. None of 'em been at the main yard since day before yesterday." Trevithick continued to regard Sheriff Hall after making his statement. Hall got the feeling he wanted to say more, or at least had more to offer if he could make up his mind to say it, but in the end he simply arose with a self-conscious smile. "I got the supply wagon. I'll take him back an' see that he's buried. As far as I'm concerned you can do it in Bannonville if you'd care to."

Hall thought for a moment before replying. "I think they got him up at the corralyard. I guess we could plant him in the local cemetery but in case your boss might not like that, you can take him back with you. And one more thing, Mister Trevithick. The next time you see Mister van der Work I'd take it kindly if you'd tell him I'd like to see him."

After Trevithick had departed Sheriff Hall brought up the old hat and resumed what he had been doing before the rangeboss walked in.

The handgun had been given perfect balance by someone, most likely an experienced gunsmith, who knew how to do that. The trigger-spring had also been filed so that almost no pressure was required to fire the weapon. Otherwise the gun looked exactly like a hundred others just like it that Mark Hall had seen.

There was nothing among the hat's contents that couldn't have been found in most other rangerider's pockets; a clasp-knife, some wornthin banknotes in small denominations, some silver coins, a soiled red bandana, a depleted sack of Bull Durham smoking-tobacco along with a little bluish packet filled with wheatstraw cigarette papers, and another little packet, this one made of heavy, oiled cardboard to protect the sulphur matches it contained.

After putting Orcutt's belongings in a box in the store-room Sheriff Hall walked up to untie the dead man's saddle animal and lead it down to the liverybarn to be watered, fed, and stalled. The liveryman, who was a notorious penny-pincher, accepted the horse, listened to the lawman's instructions for its care, and stood like a stone watching Mark Hall depart. He had not mentioned payment. The expression on Hall's face had discouraged anything like that.

The sun was sliding away. By now Sheriff Hall guessed Eliza would be pretty close to the lowest foothills. If he did not stop for the night he might arrive in town by about ten or eleven o'clock. If he was trailing the mysterious bushwhacker, he might need more time. It wasn't really old Eliza the sheriff was thinking about, except that he'd have wagered a good horse and a new saddle old Eliza would be unable to resist the temptation to follow the man with the ivory front-sight on his saddlegun.

Earlier in the day, before the interlude at the harness works, he had decided to leave town about supper-time to ride up-country hoping for a sighting. He knew better than to think he'd be able to find the killer without enough daylight to make such a sighting possible.

After his talk with Morgan Trevithick he thought it possible that van der Work and his remaining two gunfighters weren't up north just to look over the countryside. They were up there to perhaps intercept the bushwhacker and tell him that unless he completed the botched job, he might not be paid.

Maybe that wouldn't be said. Maybe van der Work would simply overlook one failure and set his hired killer on Talbot at Bertha's house to try again.

When Hall finally tucked a riding-coat under one arm, took the booted Winchester and locked the jailhouse from out front he was also pondering something else. If van der Work and his bodyguards or whatever they were, happened to still be on the north range, there was a good chance Hall would encounter them before he sighted the phantom horseman.

Evidently the dead man had split off from the others with some excuse for riding back to Bannonville, because he had been alone. Whether van der Work and the other men were bothered by his failure to return, or not, Hall had no idea. But he was fairly certain they did not know the man was dead.

They probably would not make any attempt to find him until tomorrow. Especially if they expected to meet the hired killer.

When the sheriff left town he did so by the back alley where his leaving would not be generally noticed. Not because he feared someone might spread the word of his leave-taking, but because he preferred not having any rangemen know he was out of town. What they did not know they could not pass along to anyone they encountered on their way to distant ranches. Such as van der Work or his pair of gunmen, if that's what they were. The dead man certainly had been and he had always seemed to be with the other two.

A few miles out Sheriff Hall removed his badge and pocketed it. He did not believe the phantom horseman knew him by sight but the badge would be a dead give-away, not only figuratively, but literally. A hired killer was the enemy of anyone wearing a badge.

The sun was fading, there were sheepy-clouds in the sky, the land was warm, tiny wildflowers were everywhere and the grass was flourishing. Sheriff Hall had a strong feeling for the land. He had once been told by Ben Talbot he should have been a rancher.

While there was still daylight he discerned a faint silvery reflection from just above the foothills. If the sun had been in front of the distant mountains instead of behind them the light would have been easier to see.

But what stopped Sheriff Hall near a bosk of trees was that the flashes appeared, disappeared for several minutes, then reappeared.

He rolled and lit a smoke, looped his reins and sat watching. He had been unable to make out whether there were four flashes followed after the interval by another four flashes, which would have meant Eliza Sharps was up there, or whether it was more than four flashes. They seemed to blend together in the fading light.

He killed the smoke and swung to the ground to squat in front of his horse. It had to be Eliza. The chance of it being someone else up there making mirror-signals was very, very remote.

Until Sheriff Hall thought of the bushwhacker in front of him somewhere, and van der Work behind him somewhere. *They* would have signals. If they were to rendezvous up here some place they would have. Unless of course they already knew where to rendezvous.

Hall stubbed out his smoke, stood up with thumbs hooked in his shellbelt, and hoped daylight would not fade completely before whoever was up there got down as low as the foothills where there was almost no timber and very little underbrush.

All he wanted was a good sighting. If Eliza had signalled from back up in the big timber and he was following the killer-horseman, then the bush-whacker had to be a fair distance on down-country.

He led his horse back among the trees, tethered him there and moved back where he could see along the foothills.

He did not see the phantom horseman. Late afternoon gradually faded into early dusk. With shortened vision Sheriff Hall considered riding boldly forward. The reason he abandoned that idea was that off to his left, which was westerly, a solitary rider appeared on a low knoll. He too was facing the uplands.

He was much too far away for the sheriff to make out details, but prudence suggested that the sheriff remain out of sight, because if that was who he thought it was, there would be three of them.

The sentinel, or whatever he was, did not ride down off his knoll, but eventually he dismounted to stand with his horse.

One thing was abundantly clear; whoever he was, his obvious purpose in being over there was to watch for someone who was coming down out of the mountains. To Mark Hall that meant the bushwhacker.

Sheriff Hall lost the man altogether as dusk faded into early nightfall. He thought that the sentinel must have seen the reflections. If he was one of van der Work's riders, he would be warily watching. If he was one of Ben Talbot's riders searching for cattle or perhaps a remuda of saddle stock, his curiosity would be as big as a log by the time he got back to Lard Bucket's yard.

For Mark Hall, though, the search had to end right there in the little stand of pine trees. It was a disappointment to have to head back for town with nothing to show for a long ride but some weak reflections, but there was no real alternative.

He certainly was not going to go ploughing around in darkness looking for a professional killer. Nor was he going to run the risk of running into van der Work and his pair of gun-handy hirelings.

But all the way back he felt uneasy about something. He could not pin it down. It was just one of those nagging sensations which probably had significance but Mark Hall could not interpret it.

He left his booted saddlegun and coat at the jailhouse, took the horse down to the liverybarn where a nightman took the reins, then walked thoughtfully up the north side of the road as far as Bertha Bradley's place.

When he explained to her that he thought another attempt might be made on Ben Talbot's life, her hands flew to her mouth. She was no novice about violence, which was never pleasant to anticipate, but this time it might involve her personally.

The sheriff left her in the parlour, went back to tell Ben Talbot what he had been up to, what he thought the killer was returning to do, and left his sixgun on Talbot's blanket when he returned to the parlour where Bertha took him by the arm to the kitchen, sat him down, lighted a lamp and went to work heating a meal.

As she worked she asked questions, and as he watched her work he answered them. He had a reason for no longer holding back. Unless he was very mistaken, whatever was on the way would be permanently settled before daylight returned.

When he got around to saying he had seen the phantom horseman Bertha was placing a platter of hot food before him, and frowned. She too had heard those tales. She had put no more faith in them than Mark Hall — before he saw the rider.

He grinned at her. "Wait. Just wait. If I've got this figured right you'll see him before dawn. He's no more a phantom than I am. He's the same man who's been killing people, then, for some crazy reason of his own, riding out into plain sight for them to see before he disappears into the trees or underbrush.

"Eliza says he blankets-out his sign and I know for a fact he's as elusive as a greased pig. If he wasn't he wouldn't have lived as long as he has."

"But that's taking an awful chance, Mark. Suppose one of the local rangemen accidentally rode up onto him?"

The sheriff was cutting meat so did not reply for a moment. Then all he said was: "I sure hope not. Not unless whoever runs into him is one hell of a gunman. I'll bet a good horse that bushwhacker is not only a sharpshooter with a long-gun, but pretty respectable with a short one . . . What do you call this, it's mighty good, Bertha?"

"I call it re-heated leftovers, Mark, and if you weren't as hungry as a wolf you wouldn't like it that much."

"Yes I would," he said with a twinkle. "Because you rassled it up."

She left him at the kitchen table to go searching for her late husband's sixgun. She had noticed the empty holster. When she returned she put the weapon on the table, nodded at him and returned to the parlour to keep watch toward the roadway.

11

A Real Surprise

SHERRIFF HALL hadn't been getting very much rest lately. Not since shortly after the killing of Charley Silver. He had difficulty staying awake in Bertha's house even when she occasionally brought him coffee, or sat in the darkness talking with him.

Twice when Ben Talbot rattled his bed and she departed, Sheriff Hall dozed, snapped awake, and finally began pacing through the house in his stocking feet.

The night appeared to be extraordinarily long. Time seemed to be barely passing. Finally, when Bertha brought him hot black java laced with whiskey, his drowsiness diminished, but it probably would have returned if he hadn't continued to move, to go from window to window, from door to door, to occasionally step outside to take down big, deep breaths of chilly air, and finally to visit them both in Talbot's darkened room to tell them the attempt had to be made fairly soon, otherwise the bushwhacker could not expect to reach the mountains and disappear up there before sunrise.

Talbot could not sit up but Bertha had shoved two pillows beneath his head so at least he was no longer restricted to looking at the ceiling. He was holding Hall's sixgun in a relaxed hand on his stomach. He still had a faint doubt that there was a phantom rider, but after listening to other things Mark Hall had told him, he was willing to believe that van der Work had made remarks about owning the country, and that included owning his own ranch which was an adjacency to land van der Work had already acquired.

Sheriff Hall did not spend much time in Talbot's room. Bertha did, and they quietly talked until she decided it might mitigate her restlessness if she also made rounds of the house.

In the kitchen where Sheriff Hall was slicing cold meat with a wicked-bladed clasp-knife, she said, "You could have roused the town, Mark. You could have sent for Ben's riders. Trying this by yourself and with a wounded man and a woman who hates guns, piles up the odds against your success."

He ate, smiled at her in the gloom, went on eating for a while then, as he was wiping the blade on his trousers before pocketing it he said, "I guess I didn't make it very clear, Bertha. I don't want a lot of men hidin' around town with guns in their hands, to cough, or move around on creaking boards . . . Bertha, this man is no greenhorn at his trade. His kind can get spooked if the wind blows wrong and dogs bark. I want him face-to-face. I don't want anything to scare him so's we got to do this again. You understand?"

She studied his shadowy face for a moment then moved toward the stove, drew off a cup of lukewarm coffee and handed it to him. "Yes, I understand. I suppose I do. But the idea of someone like that sneaking around out there with murder in his heart doesn't make me giddy with delight. I hope *you* understand *that*."

He understood it. "This wasn't my idea. I didn't bring Ben in here. All I wanted to do was trap this murderer. I wish it could have been done somewhere else, but it can't, not now." He did not much care for lukewarm coffee even when it had been freshly made a couple of hours earlier, so he put aside the nearly-full cup and went to the back door to lean and listen, then to raise the *tranca*, crack the door a few inches, and to finally ease out into a degree of deep darkness made deeper by the porch roof.

There was not a sound. Not for a very long time, then it sounded as though a horse was approaching from the northeast, over on the far right side of the roadway. The sound was so faint even in the complete hush that Sheriff Hall had to strain to hear it.

He held his breath, let it out and turned his head to catch sounds. Occasionally the sound diminished to the point where he could not hear it, then it would pick up again, perhaps a little closer to town because he no longer had to strain to detect it.

He sidled back into the kitchen but Bertha was out in the parlour standing to one side of a front window peeking out at the far storefronts and the empty roadway between.

He said, "There's a horse east of town."

She frowned. "East? From what I've gathered from what you've said, he would be approaching from the west, over on Mister Talbot's range. Mark; maybe it's a loose horse. Someone is always losing horses."

"Bertha, this is a ridden horse."

"Are you sure? How can you tell?"

"Horses don't usually walk along by themselves in the middle of the night. Even if they're alone, they graze as they go. I'm going back. You tell Ben what I just told you. And hope like hell it really is a loose horse."

By the time he could sidle past the door again and stand in darkness listening, the horse had come much closer. But he was not walking directly toward town now, he was making a big sashaying curve around town. So far eastward Hall had trouble hearing his hoof-falls, and that, for a fact, was about what a loose horse would do. He'd bypass the scents of ganged-together humanity. Even if he detected horse-scent, which he could do easily enough, a lot of people had sheds and corrals behind their residences where they kept animals, he still would be less likely to investigate those scents than he would be to do exactly as he seemed to be doing now — avoid contact with humans. Even sleeping ones.

After a while the sounds died out completely. Sheriff Hall went back inside, rolled and lit a smoke and sank down at the kitchen table.

Bertha came into the room with the gliding movement of a ghost. She too was not wearing shoes. When she could make out his face she moved past to lightly trail a hand across his shoulders. "Never mind. It was just one more thing we won't have to fret about."

But that was a mistake, an understandable one but nevertheless a mistake.

The passage of time bothered Sheriff Hall nearly as much as his imaginings of how his meeting with the phantom horseman would occur, and end.

When Ben Talbot rattled his bed the sheriff went back there. When Talbot expressed anxiety the sheriff inwardly agreed but outwardly made placating comments which the cowman seemed to accept; at least in the semi-darkness of his room he showed no noticeable scepticism, although as the sheriff was about to depart he said, "Mark, he don't have much time. One gunshot this close to dawn will waken half the town. And he'll still have to get away. The way folks feel right now I don't think he could do it before a posse'd overhauled him. Maybe he won't try it tonight — this morning I mean."

On that subject Sheriff Hall had almost no doubts. The man had started down out of the mountains. He was on his way. Possibly he'd been delayed by meeting van der Work out there somewhere, but sure as hell he was coming.

Bertha appeared in the doorway to whisper loudly. "Mark, there is someone out back. I saw movement from the kitchen window, at the edge of my old horse-shed."

The sheriff shouldered past on his way to the kitchen. Bertha would have followed but Ben Talbot detained her. "It wasn't a dog or maybe a loose horse?"

"I'm not sure, but it certainly was too tall for a dog and it didn't move like a horse. I'll be back," she said, and hurried to the kitchen where Sheriff Hall had the door cracked about eight inches and was peering around it in the direction of the dilapidated little shed which stood near the alley at the boundaryline of the Bradley property. As she came close he turned to whisper. "It's a man. He's behind the shed now but I saw him peek out from the north side of the shed. He must have come into your yard from the alley."

A small stone rattled on the roof, fell off and landed in a bed of red geraniums near the kitchen door. Sheriff Hall scowled as Bertha echoed his thoughts in a whisper. "That was a foolish thing to do. Unless he wants to draw attention to himself."

The lawman replied without thinking. "That kind of a son of a bitch is likely to do anything."

Bertha abruptly put her lips close to the sheriff's head and whispered. "There! Watch the door leading from the shed into the yard. See it move?"

Hall watched but detected no movement, although the door certainly could have moved. The night was at its absolute darkest and the intervening distance was at least thirty yards.

She squeezed his arm and that time he thought he could detect movement but what was more important, he heard rusty hinges grind.

He put out a rigid arm to push the woman back, drew his sixgun and held it at his side.

Another pebble rattled overhead. Bertha's breathing sounded loud in the silence which followed the noise of a falling stone. Hall shook his head. The damned fool wasn't acting the way any bushwhacker he'd ever heard of would act. They came and went in total silence, did their killing furtively and swiftly, in silence up to the moment of the killing shot, then disappeared.

The shed door was opening again, inches at a time. Hall cocked the sixgun. That brittle sound of oily steel rubbing over oily steel carried throughout the kitchen but evidently no farther because the door was being steadily pushed open.

Bertha seemed not to be breathing as Sheriff Hall slowly raised his gunhand belt-high and concentrated on what he knew would be a man-shaped silhouette appearing around the door.

This time the rock struck the back of the house, a larger rock which landed under noisy impact. Sheriff Hall's brows knitted as he waited.

Bertha suddenly said, "He's not there. Look at the ground on the north end of the shed."

For a long moment the lawman could not make out the crumpled old hat because the man's chin was on the ground as he peeked ahead toward the rear of the house. Hall shifted his belt-high sixgun and tipped it downward. At about the same time someone hissed, then made a night-bird call, a drowsy, almost mournful sound.

Bertha felt a tremor pass over Sheriff Hall seconds before he lowered the gun, eased off the hammer and leaned against the door as he began to swear in an inflectionless monotone. When he finished he said, "The damned old idiot," then leaned around the door to imitate another night-bird.

The shapeless old hat pulled back

from sight. After a moment a quiet voice spoke too softly for the sound to carry far. "Mind your manners, Sheriff. Just ease that door back more and don't do nothin' both of us will regret. You hear me?"

Hall replied brusquely. "Yes, I hear you, you darned idiot. What the hell do you think you're doing? You're goin' to scare him off."

"No I ain't. Now remember — mind your manners because I'm goin' to step into the clear. All right?"

"All right," agreed Mark Hall, sounding disgusted and annoyed as he opened the door wider, holstered his gun and looked at Bertha, who was standing with both hands clasped over her stomach, not entirely certain what was happening; but that only lasted until the tall, gaunt old ghost in greasy split-hide attire moved without a sound up onto the porch and slipped past the sheriff into the kitchen.

In poor light he looked like some faintly firewood scented ghost from thirty years earlier. She was staring as the two men growled a greeting, then Sheriff Hall closed the door, stepped to the kitchen table and turned up the lamp as he said, "What in the hell do you think you're doing, Eliza?"

Sharps pulled off his hat, smiled gallantly at Bertha and sat down at the table as though Hall had not spoken.

"Lady, I'm gawd-awful hungry an' if you'd have maybe a marrow-bone or somethin' I could gnaw on."

She shot Sheriff Hall a look. He nodded at her and moved to the opposite side of the table to sit down and glare. If there was one thing Mark Hall had learned about Eliza Sharps, it was that everything that was said around him or to him went off his back like a duck shedding water. He would not be hurried nor brow beaten into speaking until he was ready to do so.

He was not prepared to do so until Bertha set a platter of cold food in front of him, then, both elbows planted firmly as he shovelled in food, he spoke between huge mouthfuls.

"First off, he wasn't in his camp when I got back up there. He come along about a day later. I figure he was down here."

Hall nodded. "He was. He back-shot Ben Talbot. It must've been a long shot or Ben was maybe moving because while the slug knocked him off his horse, he's here in the house recovering."

Eliza nodded with his cheeks puffed out. He did not speak until they were empty. "Somethin' like that. But he was just settlin' in when someone fired a rifle from a hell of a distance. Not no carbine, rifle. Just one shot. It come up there faint but clear enough. I thought it was fired off maybe half-way down to the foothills. Anyway, he saddled up, left camp and started down-country. I figured the shot was a signal that someone wanted to see him."

"So you trailed after him."

Eliza's cheeks were full again, so, as before, he nodded his head until he was able to answer. "Yeah. Real careful though because I figured he'd shoot on sight if he saw anyone behind him."

"He probably would. Where is he now?"

Eliza chewed, swallowed, eyed the half-full platter sadly, and shoved it aside as he addressed Bertha. "It's a fine meal, ma'm. Don't get no idea I don't like it. But a man can't eat and talk at the same time. It's not mannerly, my maw used to say."

Bertha smiled and went after a whiskey bottle, two tall glasses and the water pitcher. While she was doing this Eliza continued his recitation by ignoring Hall's question and picking up where he had been interrupted.

"It was a fair ride. My horse is tough as rawhide but that black horse is tougher. When we got down a considerable distance I left my horse tied and went on afoot. I feel a lot easier'n all doin' something like that if I'm on foot."

"Where is he now, Eliza?"

Sharps ignored the question again. "Sure enough, down where there's an old burn, maybe fifteen acres of black

166

stumps and good grass, he come out into
the open where a possum-bellied big man
and two scrawnier ones was sittin' on the
ground by their horses like buck In'ians.
They talked maybe half an hour then the
strangers turned back down-country an'
the feller with the black horse turned off
more easterly, like he figured to aim for
Bannonville."

"Eliza — where is he now?"

"Well sir, Mister Hall, you know I
been at the stalkin' and skulkin' business
most of my life," Eliza said, and began
to wag his head. "I wasn't even on the
horse, I was leadin' him along without
neither of us makin'a blessed sound,
and you know what? That son of a
bitch was leanin' against a big tree in
the dark, an' I never even saw him until
he started to raise his carbine . . . Sheriff,
to my dyin' day I'll never know how he
figured out we was back there. Didn't
make a blessed sound, neither me nor
the horse, but there he was, standin'
perfectly still, on foot, with the black
horse nowhere in sight, blendin' against

that tree like he'd grown there. When I come into view he didn't raise the damned gun until we wasn't no more'n twenty feet apart. That's when I caught movement."

"Did he shoot?" Hall asked. Both he and Bertha were scarcely breathing.

"Naw, he didn't shoot. All my life I been duckin' and hidin'. That'll be my nature until I die. The second I saw that gun risin' and saw his silhouette against the tree, I dropped like a rock, rolled and nailed him to the tree with this . . . "

Eliza drew a razor-sharp fleshing-knife from the back of his belt and placed it on the table. Bertha stared as though mesmerised. The knife had a badly-worn old stag handle. The blade was easily fourteen inches long. It reflected poor candlelight.

Sheriff Hall raised his eyes from the big knife. "You killed him?"

Eliza stared back. "What would you have done, Mister Hall, if a murderin' son of a bitch was about to shoulder his gun at you? He hung against that tree like a skewered moth."

Sheriff Hall eased gently back in the chair gazing at the older man. He sighed and shot Bertha a look then said, "Eliza; by any chance did he have time to say anything?"

Sharps gazed stonily back. "That isn't even a question, Sheriff, it's a damnfool statement. Look there. From twenty feet with all my stren'th behind it because he was goin' to kill me if I didn't nail him, I stuck the man clean through an' into the tree. He didn't even have time to gasp."

"Where did the knife hit him?" Hall asked.

Eliza pushed back and stood up. "See for yourself. He's in the shed out back."

12

Setting The Trap

BERTHA chose not to leave the house, which was understandable, so Sheriff Hall followed Eliza Sharps out across the hardpan between the house and the little shed.

Most of the apprehension Mark Hall had been living with since about sundown, was now gone. There was no longer a reason to fear the night outside the house. But being in his stocking feet made him more aware of sharp small stones than he had been since childhood.

Somewhere southward a horse was shifting impatiently, a sound which could not have been heard inside the house. At the shed doorway as Eliza paused with a grin, he jerked his head in the direction of that horse-movement and softly said, "His black horse. He'd hid it in the trees but my horse scented me right up to him. Sheriff, I got a claim on that animal."

Hall gave the old scarecrow a light push. "Show me his carcass," he said. "You can have the horse as far as I'm concerned."

Eliza stepped inside the shed. What little light there was came from two open doors, one opening into the alley the other doorway the one they had just passed through. But at its best it was very poor. When Eliza paused and pointed Sheriff Hall had to strike a sulphur match to see by, and the sputtery noise of the light was accompanied by an acrid cloud of rank smoke.

Eliza leaned, grabbed cloth and held the corpse in a sitting posture. The match went out. While the lawman was lighting another one the old man said, "I could've walked past him a dozen times an' never looked twice."

Hall leaned, studied the grey, slack face and nodded his head. The mysterious horseman had no outstanding nor memorable facial characteristics. He was rather handsome, not very old, perhaps in his thirties.

Hall did not light a third match. He instead knelt, plundered the corpse's pockets and jerked his head for Eliza to follow him back to the house. But the old man said, "There's two horses tied back down the alley a ways. Mine and the black one. They been without care in a hell of a while. I'll take 'em down for the liveryman to feed, then I'll come back."

Eliza did not wait for the lawman's approval, he disappeared out into the alley.

By the time Sheriff Hall got back to the kitchen Bertha was waiting at the table, as was Ben Talbot. He was wearing an old robe that had belonged to Bertha's husband. It hung on Talbot like a tent.

Bertha got coffee, turned up the lamp and when Sheriff Hall explained about the corpse in the shed, Talbot said, "An' suppose that's not him, Mark? Suppose old Sharps nailed the wrong man?"

Hall did not think so. He hadn't see the black horse in the alley, but he knew it had been there because Eliza had told him so. As he was dumping the dead man's possessions atop the table he said, "It's him all right, Ben."

Talbot seemed to accept Hall's judgment about this, but he had something else to say. "All right. An' if he was supposed to rendezvous over on my north range with van der Work and his friends, and never showed up . . . ?"

Hall pulled up a chair, sat down and began spreading the phantom horseman's personal items across the tabletop. He stopped moving, looked straight across the table and startled both his listeners. "When Eliza first came in here to tell us he'd killed the man we were waiting for, I felt like cussing." Hall made a winters smile in the lamplight. "Now I got another idea. It came to me out there in the shed. The only thing about it I don't like is this: if van der Work was up there in the foothills to meet his bushwhacker, and the bushwhacker didn't arrive, then he's goin' to worry an' wonder a lot. Otherwise, we're goin' to take a long shot." Hall looked straight at the cowman. "In a few minutes there's goin' to be a gunshot from out back of the house, a plain-as-day attempt to kill you, Ben. We're not goin' to worry about whether it succeeded or not, we're goin' to worry about van der Work knowing the attempt was made so's he'll think his bushwhacker came directly to town from the mountains to finish what he started . . . I want van der Work right here in town."

Ben Talbot raised a hand to scratch a stubbly cheek. "Nice," he said. "Might work too, if van der Work hears about the attempt. How's he goin' to do that if he's out yonder beatin' the brush for his bushwhacker?"

Sheriff Hall did not know. "The town'll know. It's close to breakfast-time. A gunshot right now will echo all over Bannonville. Bertha and I'll meet 'em out front to say someone snuck up to the back of her house and tried to kill you in your bed. We're not goin' to say he did kill you or he didn't kill you."

The kitchen conference was interrupted by the arrival of Eliza Sharps. When Bertha admitted him to the kitchen the old pot-hunter grinned from ear to ear. "You should have seen that nightman when I walked in with two horses. He looked like he'd faint dead away. Scairt the whey out of him, me walkin' in like that an' him rubbin' his eyes from wakin' up." Eliza pulled up a chair, sat and gazed at the items on the table. He suddenly remembered something and groped inside his greasy, stained old split-hide shirt, brought forth a small bundle tied with brown string and wrapped in waterproof cloth. He pitched it among the other things on the table. "That there was in his shirt pocket. The button was gone an' it fell out when I was slingin' him over his saddle."

Sheriff Hall cut the brown string, unwrapped the bundle and caught his breath. There was not a sound as they all stared at a thick, carefully folded and tied bundle of greenbacks. The topmost one was of a high denomination. When Hall spread them all atop the table, every greenback was of that same high denomination. Ben Talbot leaned to count it aloud. They listened right up until he finished with the number "One thousan' an' nine hunnert dollars! For Chris' sake, even after sellin'-down in the autumn I never see that much money all in cash."

Eliza smiled. "Before any of you was born, I heard the killin' business paid well. But not this well. Sheriff, he sure'n hell never got that kind of money for killin' Charley Silver an' tryin' to kill Mister Talbot."

Hall had agreed with that assessment shortly after Ben had stopped counting. "Too bad he's dead. He could have explained several things. Making out like he was a ghost or something after he shot someone. Well, I guess they all got some kind of trademark, but this, my guess is that this money is what he's been paid for a lot of killings. He couldn't very well put it in a bank, could he, an' hidin' it under a rock would be takin' an even bigger risk. So he carried it with him."

Hall arose from the table as Bertha was unfolding a worn, thin square of paper. When he was about to speak Bertha spoke first while flattening the paper near the lamp. "Look at this."

Eliza's brows knitted as he stared. "What is it? Looks like someone's drawin' of four gents on horseback. Look at that first one. A man ought to be horsewhipped for lettin' his horse get that starved."

Bertha straightened slightly on her chair. She skipped Eliza and the cowman to ask Mark Hall if he knew who those horsemen were. He looked at the picture a long time before straightening up scowling. "No, ma'm. I think I've seen that . . . No, ma'm, I don't know. Do you?"

She put a finger on the rider of the bony nag. "He is Conquest." She moved her finger. "The next one is War. The third one is Famine. The fourth one — do you see where someone used a pen and ink to put a small x over the hat of that one? That is Death."

Not a word was said until Ben Talbot looked up with a furrowed brow. "That's what it was with the bushwhacker. He believed he was that Fourth Horseman. That's why he sat out there where folks could see him, then disappeared through the timber or arroyos or brush patches. Mark, he was crazy as a pet 'coon."

Eliza eased back slowly, still looking at the copy of Durer's ancient painting. "Hell, he was Death. To Charley Silver, danged near to you, Mister Talbot, an' only gawd knows how many other folks."

Pragmatic Sheriff Hall looked toward the nearest window where nightlong darkness was yielding with infinite slowness, to something else, turned back toward the table and said, "Ben, get back in your bed. Eliza, wait ten minutes after I leave then go out back, get up next

178

to the house and fire off one pistol-round into the air. Then duck back in here and stay with Bertha. It's got to look like an attempted bushwhack. I'll come up here in plain sight where folks can't help but see me. Bertha, you let me in an' close the door. Later, when folks get curious enough to come up here, you two will stay inside. I'll go out and tell them the biggest lie I've ever told." When Hall stopped speaking, he smiled coldly. "Then we wait. They may not hear about the shootin' for a long time, but when they do, you can bet a pair of new boots they'll show up in town. Van der Work's got to be convinced Ben's dead. He can't move in an' steal Ben's ranch like he did with Charley Silver, until he knows for a fact Ben is dead."

Hall left the house by the back alley. He closed the shed doors on his way, not that he expected anyone to look into the dilapidated old structure, but to prevent accidental disclosure, a wandering dog for example, or some nosy children.

By the time he reached his office dawn

was close. He was leaning to fire the kindling in the stove when a solitary gunshot sounded up toward the north end of town on the east side. He finished getting the fire going, smiled coldly to himself and waited a moment before appearing in the roadside doorway.

Across the road the general store's proprietor and his elderly clerk with the black sleeve-protectors were standing in chilly newday light peering northward. Down at the smithy where someone was in the act of removing the large front panels that covered the open front of the shed, the man was still balancing one of the panels as he too froze motionless looking northward.

On the same side of the road as the jailhouse Hank McHenry stepped forth holding the apron he'd been about to put on when the gunshot sounded. Hank called across the road where Ike Cameron was out front of his gunshop holding a cup of coffee.

"What the hell was that?"

Ike answered shortly. "A gunshot.

What did it sound like?"

"Where from?"

Ike shrugged. "Up the road on this side. Maybe up near the Widder Bradley's place."

Sheriff Hall re-set his hat, took a sawed-off shotgun from the wall rack and walked out into the roadway. More people appeared. The cranky old man who owned the pool-room called out. "Get out of the centre of the road, Sheriff. He could hit you wearin' a blindfold, for Chris'sake!"

Hall angled to the plankwalk and nodded to the old man as he continued northward. Every eye was on him as he unslung the scattergun from the crook of an arm and held it in both hands as he approached Bertha's house.

13

'Three Men . . .'

THEY were waiting in the parlour. When Bertha opened the door Sheriff Hall smiled at her, looked past at the cowman and said, "How do you feel?"

Talbot hadn't gone back to bed. He was still attired in the bathrobe that hung on him like a tent. His reply was rueful. "Like a man sittin' on a keg of dynamite."

They stood at the front windows watching the townsmen where they came together in small groups, talking, occasionally gesturing in the direction of the Bradley house, and evidently waiting for the sheriff to emerge.

He took his time. Bertha made coffee. When she was in the kitchen and the others were watching from the windows as

Bannonville's residents were increasingly congregating across the road, Sheriff Hall also went to the kitchen. She turned as he walked in. "Are you hungry? I fed the others." She paused, then as she faced the stove again she also said, "That old man must have worms. I never saw anyone eat like he can."

Hall sat at the table watching her. "You're probably the only woman who's fed him a decent meal in twenty years."

She spoke again while her back was still to him. "He washed that big knife in my sink."

Hall shoved his thick legs out and savoured the aroma of heating coffee. "He's lived hard all his life, Bertha. He wouldn't do anything to upset you, if he knew it would."

She turned, large, strong and solid. "I know. He means well. When I was a child I remember seeing men like that — more Indian than white, more wild than tame. But it's been a long time. I thought that by now they were all gone."

He changed the subject. "How is Ben doing?"

"Like I told you, Mark, he's not young but he's as healthy as a horse. So far there's no sign of infection. He'll be able to go home in a wagon within a few days. But no horsebacking or hard work for a month."

Hall laughed as he stood up. "I'd like to see his face when you tell him that. Well, I've been in here long enough. They'll be bustin' with curiosity out there."

She returned to the parlour with him and at the door when Eliza said, "About time, Sheriff, couple of them been itchin' to come over and bang on the door," Bertha Bradley brushed his arm with her fingers and told him to be careful, that they'd wait for him to return.

Eliza was correct. No sooner had Sheriff Hall appeared with the shotgun in his arm than people called to him. He shook his head, acting very solemn, and went southward without answering questions.

Hank McHenry and Ike Cameron were standing together over in front of the harness shop. They said nothing as they watched the sheriff walk southward, but when he angled across the road toward the jailhouse McHenry said, "Well, he don't look pleased, does he?"

The gunsmith agreed with that. "No, an' more'n likely that means somethin' bad happened over at the widder's place. You want to go over there and knock on the door?"

McHenry put on the apron he'd been holding up to now, tied it and shook his head. "No. An' neither do you. If he'd wanted our help he'd have asked for it."

Each man returned to his place of business, the little clutches of townsmen eventually went about their business, and as Mark Hall was sitting at his desk in the jailhouse office drinking coffee, van der Work's rangeboss appeared in the doorway.

Hall motioned toward a chair, went after another cup of coffee and handed it to Trevithick without saying a word until he was back in his chair; then he said, "How long you been in town, Mister Trevithick?"

The reply was short. "Just long enough to leave my horse at the liverybarn and walk up here."

You must have left before sunrise to reach Bannonville so early in the day."

Trevithick looked into his cup before raising it. "I did. It was darker'n the inside of a boat, and cold." Trevithick drank briefly, lowered the cup and looked directly at the sheriff. "The liveryman said there'd been a shootin' just before I rode in."

Hall nodded. "There was. Up at the lady's house where Ben Talbot is bein' looked after."

Trevithick continued to look at Mark Hall. "Someone sure wants him dead."

Hall inclined his head again, drank coffee and put the cup aside. "Maybe the same man tried to kill him before."

"Any worthwhile sign?"

"No. But there never has been when that bushwhacker shows up. Was Mister van der Work at the ranch when you left this morning?"

"No. An' that sort of troubles me. I haven't seen hide nor hair of him in three days. Or those fellers he keeps with him. I need to get some orders from him. Damned cattle are still comin' and we're workin' ourselves into early graves tryin' to count them in, then find feed for 'em."

Sheriff Hall's gaze never left Morgan Trevithick's face. He made shrewd judgments of every expression that shadowed the man's face. In the end he felt more certain than ever that van der Work's rangeboss was just that and nothing more. He asked if Trevithick had buried Wood Orcutt and got a glum nod.

"Yeah. We buried him, an' no one shed any tears, but now there's talk among the riders."

"What kind of talk?"

"About Mister van der Work, the other two men who stay with him everywhere, and what in hell is goin' on. You know

TFH13

how talk gets started."

Hall knew. He watched the lanky man put aside the cup and get to his feet. Trevithick offered a wan smile at the door when he said, "I'm sorry about Talbot. But what I figured was that Mister van der Work might be in town."

Sheriff Hall shook his head. "Not that I know of."

The rangeboss's smile faded. "He's not. The liveryman said he hadn't put up no horses except two for some old pot-hunter in several days. That means I got to ride all over hell to find him. If he comes along, Sheriff, I'd appreciate it if you'd tell him I got to talk to him real bad." As Hall arose nodding about that, Trevithick reiterated what he'd said earlier. "I'm real sorry about Mister Talbot," and walked out into the sunshine leaving the sheriff gazing after him. Evidently something Hall had said had convinced the rangeboss that Talbot had been killed.

To show himself, and to hopefully

draw attention to himself and away from the Bradley house, Hall walked down to the liverybarn.

The proprietor was out back where two sets of corrals adjoined. One set belonged to him. The others were public corrals, pens for livestock of strangers who might be passing through.

The lawman did not go out there until he'd strolled the runway looking for a black horse. He found him dozing on a full belly in a shadowy stall. He wasn't truly black, he was a seal-brown colour, but from a distance he would look black. In some cases people even referred to seal-browns as black horses. No genuine horseman ever did, but genuine horsemen were few and far between, particularly in towns.

There was a neat little spidery brand on the animal's left shoulder. A Mex brand. Unlike brands north of the border which were commonly made by hot irons consisting of straight lines, many brands from below the border were artistic, had curves, and were applied by men who almost never blurred their marks.

While the sheriff was leaning on the low door looking at the dozing horse the liveryman came shuffling in from out back with a carelessly coiled rope around one arm. He walked up, looked in, pursed his lips and said, "Valuable animal. Breedy, and look at them shoulders and that chest. You won't believe it, but that old buckskin pot-hunter who peddles meat around town brought him in. Real early this morning. Hour or two before daylight. This horse an' a big stout bay with a little age on him."

Having said this much the liveryman leaned close to the lawman and half-whispered the rest of it. "Stole him sure as hell. His kind never have enough money to buy this kind of an animal. He's got to still be around somewhere, Sheriff. You know him by sight. He's been peddlin' game around here for years. I don't recollect his name, but you know who I mean."

Hall straightened up off the low door. "Yeah, I know him. Eliza Sharps."

"That's it. That's the name. I just couldn't remember it but that's it."

Hall was turning away as he said, "I'll look around for him."

The liveryman suddenly got nervous. "Don't tell him I said anythin' about this horse. My nightman said the old scoundrel had a knife on the back of his shellbelt long enough to go through a man with six inches to spare."

Sheriff Hall agreed. "Not a word, an' you can return the favour. Did you see that big feller ridin' a silver outfit who was in town a few days back?"

"Yep. Sure did. Mister van der Work."

"If he shows up in town today let me know," said Hall, and in response to the look of inquisitiveness he added a little more. "His rangeboss is lookin' for him."

Back out in the sunshine Sheriff Hall sauntered back up toward his jailhouse office again. He was stopped several times and each time he told the same story. "Someone snuck up in back of Bertha Bradley's house for a final shot at Ben Talbot." Adding 'final shot' was something that had occurred to him about the time Morgan Trevithick had been at the jailhouse. He hoped it would be interpreted the way he wanted it to be, and apparently it was because he hadn't been back in his office ten minutes when the harness-maker and gunsmith walked in.

The older men were as solemn as owls. McHenry said, "Folks are wonderin' why you aren't in the saddle after that murderin' son of a bitch."

Hall leaned with both hands behind his head. "*Viejos*, you can catch more flies with sugar then with vinegar," he said.

The gunsmith's eyes narrowed slightly and he remained silent but Hank McHenry didn't. "Not settin' in here."

Hall gestured. "There's coffee in the pot. Cold by now but it's wet."

The harness-maker began to bristle. He probably would have launched into a tirade but his companion punched him under the ribs with a bony elbow.

Hall affected not to notice this as the harness-maker flinched and put a look of puzzled disapproval on his friend.

Cameron went over to tip cold coffee into a cup and turned back to ask a question. "You're up to somethin' aren't you? Don't look innocent to me, Sheriff. I seen that look a hunnert times on folks who was being sly. It's all right with us. It's just that everyone on both sides of the road is makin' hard talk about you stayin' in town while that assassin is hightailing it."

Hall continued to lean back regarding the pair of older men. "You remember that talk a while back about a phantom rider appearin' then disappearing?" he asked, and this time the harness-maker spoke first.

"You're not goin' to tell us it was that feller who killed Ben, are you? Sheriff, for Chris'sake, if folks heard you say somethin' like that they'd go to the Town Council to get you removed for being crazy."

"Hank, I didn't say he killed Ben, I

asked if you remembered those stories about him."

"Sure. Everyone remembers. The more they got told around the better they got. I heard a passenger lyin' over for the mornin' stage up at the saloon say that he'd heard about the mysterious horseman, and knew for a blessed fact that back in Missouri when he was a youngster they caught one of them fellers, killed him and folks who knew about such things drove a wood stake through his chest before he was buried. Sheriff, I sure hope Ike is right about you bein' up to something, because if you walk out of here and go over to the store or up to the saloon and talk about that ghost rider, the whole damned sky is goin' to fall on you."

After the old men had departed Sheriff Hall made a fresh pot of coffee but did not fire up the stove. He simply put the pot on the burner before dropping his hat back on and leaving the jailhouse on his way across the road and up as far as the Bradley house.

Over in front of the general store a few loafers nodded but only one spoke. "Sheriff, that bushwhacker ain't goin' to hang around town waitin' for you."

Farther along, near the saloon, two dusty rangemen were freeing their animals to ride out of town. One of them grinned as the lawman walked by. "Talbot's riders ain't goin' to like it, you not beatin' the brush for his killer." The man kept on grinning until Mark Hall was out of earshot, then the grin winked out, the cowboy put a malevolent glare up where the sheriff was walking, and spoke to his companion.

"I been comin' into this country to ride for five years, an' I've seen him clean out the pool-hall an' the saloon without even wearin' a gun. He's sure as hell got punky. Never even looked at me nor answered back."

His companion had finished getting ready to mount, backed his animal clear and was reaching for the horn with his left foot in the stirrup when he replied. "I don't know, Jess. This is my first year up here, but I've heard stories about him, an' just now when he was walkin' past I seen his face pretty good. If I was you I wouldn't bait him like that again."

The rider named Jess snorted derisively, swung up and led the ride out of town southward at a dead walk.

Just before Sheriff Hall raised a fist to rattle Bertha Bradley's door he turned to watch the progress of those two rangemen until they were abreast of the liverybarn, then he knocked. He liked the idea of them riding out to Lard Bucket and stirring up Ben's men.

Bertha appeared, wiping her hands on an apron. As he moved inside and she closed the door she said, "They're eating again."

He looked down into her face. "It's noon, Bertha."

"But they haven't stopped since breakfast. Especially Mister Sharps. Sheriff, he really does need worming."

A quick rattle of someone's bony knuckles behind them startled Bertha and caused Hall to twist from the waist as the knocking continued. He stepped over, opened the door and Ike Cameron, whose insistent knocking had sounded peremptory, looked calmly at Sheriff Hall as he spoke.

"Did you want to see that possum-bellied gent that rides a silver saddle?" Cameron jerked his head. "They're comin' toward town from the north roadway. Him an' three others."

Hall's brows pulled inward and downward. "*Three* men with him?"

"Yep. Three."

14

End Of The Trail

AFTER Ike Cameron had departed Sheriff Hall returned to the kitchen, told the others what Cameron had reported, and Ben Talbot, who was drinking hot beef broth from a bottle, looked quizzically upwards. "Three riders with him? From what I've figured out there should be only two, because you blew one of his bodyguards out of his shirt over at the harness shop."

Hall was frowning when he murmured, "Trevithick, his rangeboss? He told me he had to talk to van der Work. He said he'd have to find him."

Eliza wiped his mouth on a greasy cuff and pushed back from the table. First, he cast a roguish wink at Bertha, then he stood up to hitch his weapons-belt into place, then he said, "Well, gents. This much I can tell you for a fact. They didn't see me. Even if they could've seen in the dark, I rode over east until they couldn't even hear me — no one could who was west of the road — then I headed for town, an' no one followed me. I know they didn't. I been all my life ridin' with one ear cocked back."

Sharps paused briefly then moved towards the back door. "I'll slip around until I can see up yonder." He departed before anyone spoke. They couldn't have dissuaded him it they had tried.

Bertha handed Sheriff Hall a cup of hot coffee, which he held without raising it as he returned to the parlour where he could see southward fairly well, but his northward view was obstructed by buildings.

He tasted the coffee. The others came into the parlour and Bertha cracked the front door a few inches, pulled back to close it and made a quiet statement: "They're in place, Sheriff."

He turned. "Who's in place?"

"Your friends. Look across the road. Mister McHenry's on the roof of the harness works. Come over here where you can lean out and look southward. Mister Cameron is standing in front of the dog-trot between his shop and the next building below."

Mark Hall put the cup aside, crossed to the door and looked out. There was no sign of Ike. He looked elsewhere, caught a faint movement along the upper false front of the harness shop, turned swiftly to look northward where he saw four riders walking their horses toward town, then closed the door as Eliza's nasal voice sounded from the kitchen doorway.

"There's four of 'em, for a fact, Sheriff, an' I'm fairly certain one of 'em's that feller I saw settin' on a little knoll facin' the mountains yestiddy. The only other one that makes a swathe is the big, pot-bellied man ridin' a chestnut horse an' a silver-mounted saddle."

Sheriff Hall retrieved his cup and drained it, then handed it to Bertha as he walked to the doorway where Eliza moved aside to allow him to pass, and when the others heard the back door softly close Ben Talbot swore softly and went after his boots, shirt and britches.

Bertha was torn between rushing after Ben to admonish him against the exertion of dressing, and watching the front roadway for some sign of Mark Hall.

Eliza returned briefly to the kitchen, came back with his cheeks pouched like those of a chipmunk, grinned at Bertha and spoke awkwardly around a mouth full of food. "That possum-bellied gent is ridin' into a surprise, wouldn't you say, ma'm? I'll tell you somethin' else: If I remembered womenfolk could cook like you do, I would likely have turned my horses loose, soap-washed my clothes, got sheared and shaved an' gone to courting."

Into the moments of silence which followed Eliza's statement came the faint but persistent sound of ridden horses.

Eliza had to swallow three times to get his mouthful disposed of as he went to the front window. He chuckled. "That feller on the roof popped up his head then yanked it down like a prairie dog."

Sheriff Hall came soundlessly into the parlour from out back. As he was starting to speak Ben Talbot emerged from his darkened room fully dressed and wearing his shellbelt. He had Sheriff Hall's sixgun in the holster.

The sheriff was looking at Talbot when he said, "The third one is Trevithick, his rangeboss."

Talbot did not comment. He crossed the room toward the window but was intercepted by Bertha whose hand on his arm was firm. "You'll start bleeding if you haven't already."

He did not dispute this but his answer indicated how his thoughts were running. "Bertha, right now, at the risk of some bleeding, it's more important to me to see that son of a bitch settled up with, because if it don't happen today, if he rides out of this, sure as hell he'll get my ranch an' dance on my grave."

The first of the riders to come into

view from the parlour window was van der Work, which Mark Hall accepted as the natural position of someone with the big man's dominating personality. Directly behind him was Morgan Trevithick. He was riding slightly apart from the other two men and his expression showed equal parts weariness and disillusionment.

The other two men who had been riding with van der Work slouched in silence, beard-stubbled, faded-looking with scuffed boots, dusty old sweat-stained hats and weathered, lined faces set in expressions blasted out of hard lives and hazardous living. Those two had evidently begun to feel wary about the time they entered Bannonville. They had reason; the roadway was empty, only a handful of people were abroad and several of them faded into doorways at sight of the riders. By now everyone knew van der Work by sight. They had all heard disquieting stories about him, and while it was possible they might have reserved their judgments until he appeared in the centre of the roadway with three capable-looking armed men for companions, they now instinctively chose prudence over curiosity and made themselves scarce.

Sheriff Hall waited until they were directly in front of Bertha's house where the big man turned his head and stared. He stepped to the door, lifted the latch and stopped in the opening. Van der Work saw him, lifted his rein-hand, sat a moment regarding Hall, then reined toward the tie-rack as he said, "G'day, Sheriff."

Hall nodded. "Howdy." His glance touched each of the men still in the centre of the roadway, returned to the big man and remained there.

Van der Work leaned slightly to shift weight in the saddle as he spoke again. "I was going on down to your office."

Hall's lips pulled back in a death's-head smile. "Somethin' I can help you with?"

Van der Work jerked his head. "Morgan told me someone killed Ben Talbot."

Hall's strained smile remained. "Some-one sure wanted him out of the way."

Van der Work nodded about that, straightened slightly in an effort to see beyond Hall into the house, but Hall's big-boned frame pretty well prevented this, so he sat back down as he said, "When's the funeral, Sheriff?"

Hall's smile was diminishing. "I don't know. Care to look at the body, Mister van der Work?"

The large man shook his head. "No need. I'm sorry he's dead but we hardly knew each other." Van der Work's rein-hand was rising when the lawman spoke again, causing the hand to pause in mid-air.

"If you don't care to look at the body maybe there's something else you might want to see. We found it in Talbot's pocket and it mentions you and somethin' to do with land."

Van der Work sat like stone for a moment, eased his rein-hand down and twisted from the waist as he spoke to his companions. "Hal, hold my horse. The

205

rest of you go on down to the liverybarn, get some grain and water for the horses and I'll meet you at the cafe directly."

Only Morgan Trevithick had deep creases in his forehead as Hal Jones rode over, swung off and accepted the reins from his employer, but Trevithick had no opportunity to speak if he'd intended to because the other hard-faced man nudged him with a stirrup and started southward.

Hal Jones leaned on the tie-rack holding two sets of reins while watching his employer enter the house. He seemed more relaxed than he'd been before his boss had spoken to the local lawman. In fact, after the door closed on van der Work, Jones settled his back against the tie-rack and went to work manufacturing a smoke.

Van der Work was ten feet past the roadside door when the sheriff closed it. Van der Work's small pale eyes showed no surprise when they settled on Bertha, nor when they settled on Eliza Sharps who was gazing straight

206

back, but when Ben Talbot walked into the parlour from his dark bedroom the large man's eyes opened very wide, he seemed not to be able to breathe for a second, and he was clearly overwhelmed, not altogether because what Morgan had told him was obviously untrue, but also because if Talbot wasn't dead, and a second gunshot attempt had been made to kill him, then . . .

Sheriff Hall leaned, lifted away the big man's sixgun and used it to prod him gently in the ribs with as he jerked his head in the direction of the kitchen door.

Van der Work turned to speak. Behind him Ben Talbot cocked a handgun. It was an unmistakable sound. Sheriff Hall looked swiftly past van der Work at Talbot but Eliza had already very casually stepped between the cowmen so that Talbot could not fire.

Hall nudged the heavy man again, a little harder this time, and herded him ahead through the kitchen, out the rear door and back to that dilapidated small shed. As he urged the large man to enter, van der Work looked questioningly around and said, "You mean to lock me in here?"

Hall nudged him again, hard enough to make the big man wince. "No. Just walk in there. Fine, now go over and take a good look at him. Move, damn it!"

Van der Work moved. It was not possible to see his face except in profile when he was looking down at the dead assassin. Sheriff Hall holstered his weapon and blocked the doorway as he said, "How much did you pay him for killin' Charley Silver?"

Van der Work acted as though he had not heard. For a long while he stood gazing at the dead man, then he seemed to rally as he looked toward Mark Hall. "Who is he?"

Hall looked stonily back, unsure about what he should have expected, but not surprised that van der Work would take this position. "You tell me. You hired him, you paid him; you didn't go riding over the north range to look it over, you

208

rode to the foothills to meet him."

Van der Work was fully recovered from his shock. He slowly wagged his head at Sheriff Hall. "I never saw that man before in my life. Is that all you wanted to show me; how about something you said you found in Mister Talbot's pocket?"

Sheriff Hall did not reply for a long time, then his expression was disdainful. "You're a lousy actor, van der Work. You saw Ben. You know there was a gunshot last night outside the house. Trevithick knew it because I told him an' he told you. You may have bluffed your way other times, but not this time." He jutted his chin in the direction of the corpse. "You saw the wound."

Van der Work involuntarily looked back and downward. "A lot of blood, Sheriff. It's dark in here."

Hall's eyes narrowed on the large man, on the shadowy corpse and back to the large man, and he lied. "It wasn't a bullet that bled him out and he told a pretty interestin' story before he cashed in."

Van der Work continued to stare at the corpse. His jaw muscles rippled, which Hall could not discern in the gloom. He finally spoke, his tone slower and less confident. "Whoever he is, he had to lie because I never saw him before — "

"You paid him, Mister van der Work. You had secret meetings with him. He maybe read some fairy tales some time because he put in a dramatic appearance in plain sight but out of gun-range after his killings. When I find out more about him sure as hell I'll find out he did that at other murders. Right now, I'm goin' to waltz you down to the jailhouse, lock you in an' feed the key to a turkey. When you've thought it all out you can let me know. This time I'll bet a lot of money you rot in prison."

The large man faced forward again. "I'll get my lawyer up here from Denver. You can't hold me. I told you, that man is a stranger to me."

Sheriff Hall smiled and expanded his lie. "You saw the old man in hunting clothes in the house; his name is Eliza

Sharps. He lives back yonder in the mountains. He spied on your bushwhacker, kept track of everything he did . . . And he was with me when your killer told us about your scheme to buy up adjoining ranges by having him kill the owners."

Hall knew almost before he had finished speaking that he might have gone too far. Van der Work was staring at him. When he spoke his voice was stronger again, more confident as he said, "He didn't tell you any such damned thing because he didn't know my plans." The large man jerked a contemptuous thumb rearward. "Who would confide in someone like that?"

Sheriff Hall stood gazing directly at the large man in stony silence. He waited until van der Work's expression subtly changed, then smiled without a trace of humour. Ignoring the large man's incriminating outburst he asked what the mysterious horseman's name was.

Van der Work's mouth was clamped

closed. He looked steadily back without making a sound.

Hall pointed. "He packs a pretty elegant sixgun. Ivory stock and all. His Winchester is fitted for a night-shooting with an ivory front-sight. Some — where he's got a mouth-organ. Maybe up at his camp. He's good at making music with it . . . What was his name?"

The big man's expression remained obdurate.

Hall stepped aside. "Walk back toward the house. If you got a belly-gun I hope you try to use it. *Now walk!*"

They were mid-way to the house when van der Work finally unlocked his jaws. "Sheriff?"

"What?"

"There is five thousand dollars in my saddle bags. New greenbacks. I'll knock you down and you won't recover until I'm gone."

Hall leaned and gave the large man a shove without speaking.

In the kitchen Eliza, Bertha and Ben were waiting. They saw all they had to see in van der Work's face when he halted with Mark Hall behind him. At that moment a heavy gloved fist rattled the parlour door. Bertha jumped. Eliza rolled his eyes around to the sheriff. "I expect that'll be his horse-holder, Mister Hall."

Eliza was reaching in back for his big knife when Hall growled at him. "Stay right here. Keep an eye on this one." As Hall left the kitchen Bertha Bradley's hand flew to her lips and remained there.

Eliza's guess had been correct. When Hall opened the door Hal Jones was standing there pulling off his riding-gloves. He looked at the slightly taller, thick man with a testy expression. "I would like to talk to Mister van der Work," he said, tucking the gloves under his shellbelt and folding them over. When Sheriff Hall did not speak the gunman added a little more. "Our horses need water and a bait of grain." He started forward as he finished speaking. When Hall made no move to clear the doorway, Jones stopped, colour rose into his face and he took one short rearward step with both hands at his sides. He matched Hall stare for stare, and waited.

Without any warning there was a deafening explosion from the kitchen followed in seconds by another one.

Sheriff Hall was beginning to whip around when he saw Hal Jones' right arm moving. Hall was slightly off balance as he struck the door jamb and covered the five feet separating him from Jones. It was not a direct blow, otherwise Hall's considerable weight would probably have knocked Jones backwards to the ground, but it was strong enough to knock Jones sideways and staggering. The cocked gun exploded between them, tore up a gout of hardpan soil complete with flying particles and dust.

Jones was still trying to get untracked enough to regain his balance when Sheriff Hall reached for his holstered Colt. There was another gunshot, this one making a high-pitched, more incisive sound. Jones was straightened up under impact but for a moment he did not appear to have been hit. Hall's gun was up and cocked when Hal Jones turned very slowly, looking puzzled about something, saw the kneeling older man in front of a dog-trot with a long-barrelled old frontiersman's rifle snugged to his shoulder southward from the Bradley house. Then he fell.

Sheriff Hall looked down, saw puddling scarlet, kicked Jones' gun into the roadway, eased down the dog of his own weapon and was holstering it when a high yell boomed from across the road and upwards somewhere.

"Ike, you old rascal, you nailed him plumb centre!"

Cameron got stiffly upright from his kneeling position, ignored the saddle-maker's shout, and leaned on the rifle waiting for Sheriff Hall to speak.

He did not say a word; he turned back into the house, strode to the kitchen where Eliza was fanning a fainted Bertha Bradley with his disreputable old hat and

Ben Talbot was sitting at the table staring at a hole in the wall above the wood-stove. When Hall entered he turned back very slowly, tossed the sixgun atop the table and said, "Take back this damned weapon, Sheriff. I didn't no more than barely clear the holster with the barrel tipped, and the thing went off."

Hall retrieved his gun, tossed the other one atop the table and looked over where Henry van der Work was lying. Eliza looked up from his fanning. "He's lyin' on it, the damned fool."

Hall leaned, hoisted the dead man, picked up the little under-and-over belly-gun, opened it and ejected one unspent shell. The barrel of the little weapon was almost large enough for a man to put his finger into. In a room no larger than Bertha's kitchen it was the match of any other handgun.

Ben leaned from the chair staring at the dead man. "He was facing the stove. Bertha and Eliza were behind him. I was more to one side. He was reaching inside his coat in front. I couldn't see much more'n that but alarm bells was goin' off in my head so I was moving over to grab him when he turned with that little gun and fired darn near point-blank at me." Talbot pointed. "That's where the slug struck, eighteen inches to one side of me. How in the hell could it have happened like that, Mark?"

Eliza answered. "Mister Talbot, don't never question Providence . . . One of you find the whiskey bottle in the cupboard. She's plumb lost to the world. An' she's heavier'n I figured."

Someone called diffidently from the parlour. Sheriff Hall left it to Ben Talbot to find the whiskey and went out there. Ike Cameron was still carrying the long-barrelled rifle. He was as solemn as an owl. "I wouldn't have chanced it with a factory made gun, Sheriff."

Hall let go a long, ragged breath, eyed the long-rifle and nodded his head. It wasn't the gun, it was the eyesight of a man as grizzled and grey as the mountains. He finally reached and roughly slapped Cameron on the shoulder. "You did right. I'm obliged."

Cameron smiled slightly. "They got the other two down at the saloon. An' there's somethin' else, Sheriff. Pretty serious."

Hall's brows knitted. He was just beginning to believe it was over. All but untangling the mess left behind by van der Work, except for eventually getting the identification of the phantom horseman; but he really did not have much to do with legal ramifications, that was why there were legal authorities who did not pack guns and wore nice black suits with button shoes instead of boots . . .

He was waiting but evidently Cameron was unwilling to volunteer anything, so Hall helped him along. "What the hell else can happen, Ike? What is it?"

"We don't have a doctor in town, Sheriff."

Hall's frown deepened. "Who is it? What happened?"

"Hank fell off the roof of his harness works and busted his leg. I got him on his bed but he's in misery, Sheriff."

THE END

Other titles in the
Linford Western Library:

TOP HAND
Wade Everett

The Broken T was big. But no ranch is big enough to let a man hide from himself.

GUN WOLVES OF LOBO BASIN
Lee Floren

The Feud was a blood debt. When Smoke Talbot found the outlaws who gunned down his folks he aimed to nail their hide to the barn door.

SHOTGUN SHARKEY
Marshall Grover

The westbound coach carrying the indomitable Larry and Stretch headed for a shooting showdown.

FIGHTING RAMROD
Charles N. Heckelmann

Most men would have cut their losses, but Frazer counted the bullets in his guns and said he'd soak the range in blood before he'd give up another inch of what was his.

LONE GUN
Eric Allen

Smoke Blackbird had been away too long. The Lequires had seized the Blackbird farm, forcing the Indians and settlers off, and no one seemed willing to fight! He had to fight alone.

THE THIRD RIDER
Barry Cord

Mel Rawlins wasn't going to let anything stand in his way. His father was murdered, his two brothers gone. Now Mel rode for vengeance.

ARIZONA DRIFTERS
W. C. Tuttle

When drifting Dutton and Lonnie Steelman decide to become partners they find that they have a common enemy in the formidable Thurston brothers.

TOMBSTONE
Matt Braun

Wells Fargo paid Luke Starbuck to outgun the silver-thieving stagecoach gang at Tombstone. Before long Luke can see the only thing bearing fruit in this eldorado will be the gallows tree.

HIGH BORDER RIDERS
Lee Floren

Buckshot McKee and Tortilla Joe cut the trail of a border tough who was running Mexican beef into Texas. They stopped the smuggler in his tracks.

BRETT RANDALL, GAMBLER
E. B. Mann

Larry Day had the choice of running away from the law or of assuming a dead man's place. No matter what he decided he was bound to end up dead.

THE GUNSHARP
William R. Cox

The Eggerleys weren't very smart. They trained their sights on Will Carney and Arizona's biggest blood bath began.

THE DEPUTY OF SAN RIANO
Lawrence A. Keating and
Al. P. Nelson

When a man fell dead from his horse, Ed Grant was spotted riding away from the scene. The deputy sheriff rode out after him and came up against everything from gunfire to dynamite.

FARGO: MASSACRE RIVER
John Benteen

The ambushers up ahead had now blocked the road. Fargo's convoy was a jumble, a perfect target for the insurgents' weapons!

SUNDANCE: DEATH IN THE LAVA
John Benteen

The Modoc's captured the wagon train and its cargo of gold. But now the halfbreed they called Sundance was going after it . . .

HARSH RECKONING
Phil Ketchum

Five years of keeping himself alive in a brutal prison had made Brand tough and careless about who he gunned down . . .

FARGO: PANAMA GOLD
John Benteen

With foreign money behind him, Buckner was going to destroy the Panama Canal before it could be completed. Fargo's job was to stop Buckner.

FARGO: THE SHARPSHOOTERS
John Benteen

The Canfield clan, thirty strong were raising hell in Texas. Fargo was tough enough to hold his own against the whole clan.

PISTOL LAW
Paul Evan Lehman

Lance Jones came back to Mustang for just one thing — revenge! Revenge on the people who had him thrown in jail.

HELL RIDERS
Steve Mensing

Wade Walker's kid brother, Duane, was locked up in the Silver City jail facing a rope at dawn. Wade was a ruthless outlaw, but he was smart, and he had vowed to have his brother out of jail before morning!

DESERT OF THE DAMNED
Nelson Nye

The law was after him for the murder of a marshal — a murder he didn't commit. Breen was after him for revenge — and Breen wouldn't stop at anything . . . blackmail, a frameup . . . or murder.

DAY OF THE COMANCHEROS
Steven C. Lawrence

Their very name struck terror into men's hearts — the Comancheros, a savage army of cutthroats who swept across Texas, leaving behind a blood-stained trail of robbery and murder.

SUNDANCE: SILENT ENEMY
John Benteen

A lone crazed Cheyenne was on a personal war path. They needed to pit one man against one crazed Indian. That man was Sundance.

LASSITER
Jack Slade

Lassiter wasn't the kind of man to listen to reason. Cross him once and he'll hold a grudge for years to come — if he let you live that long.

LAST STAGE TO GOMORRAH
Barry Cord

Jeff Carter, tough ex-riverboat gambler, now had himself a horse ranch that kept him free from gunfights and card games. Until Sturvesant of Wells Fargo showed up.

GUNSLINGER'S RANGE
Jackson Cole

Three escaped convicts are out for revenge. They won't rest until they put a bullet through the head of the dirty snake who locked them behind bars.

RUSTLER'S TRAIL
Lee Floren

Jim Carlin knew he would have to stand up and fight because he had staked his claim right in the middle of Big Ike Outland's best grass.

THE TRUTH ABOUT SNAKE RIDGE
Marshall Grover

The troubleshooters came to San Cristobal to help the needy. For Larry and Stretch the turmoil began with a brawl and then an ambush.

WOLF DOG RANGE
Lee Floren

Will Ardery would stop at nothing, unless something stopped him first — like a bullet from Pete Manly's gun.

DEVIL'S DINERO
Marshall Grover

Plagued by remorse, a rich old reprobate hired the Texas Troubleshooters to deliver a fortune in greenbacks to each of his victims.

GUNS OF FURY
Ernest Haycox

Dane Starr, alias Dan Smith, wanted to close the door on his past and hang up his guns, but people wouldn't let him.

DONOVAN
Elmer Kelton

Donovan was supposed to be dead. Uncle Joe Vickers had fired off both barrels of a shotgun into the vicious outlaw's face as he was escaping from jail. Now Uncle Joe had been shot — in just the same way.

CODE OF THE GUN
Gordon D. Shirreffs

MacLean came riding home, with saddle tramp written all over him, but sewn in his shirt-lining was an Arizona Ranger's star.

GAMBLER'S GUN LUCK
Brett Austen

Gamblers seldom live long. Parker was a hell of a gambler. It was his life — or his death . . .

ORPHAN'S PREFERRED
Jim Miller

Sean Callahan answers the call of the Pony Express and fights Indians and outlaws to get the mail through.

DAY OF THE BUZZARD
T. V. Olsen

All Val Penmark cared about was getting the men who killed his wife.

THE MANHUNTER
Gordon D. Shirreffs

Lee Kershaw knew that every Rurale in the territory was on the lookout for him. But the offer of $5,000 in gold to find five small pieces of leather was too good to turn down.

RIFLES ON THE RANGE
Lee Floren

Doc Mike and the farmer stood there alone between Smith and Watson. There was this moment of stillness, and then the roar would start. And somebody would die . . .

HARTIGAN
Marshall Grover

Hartigan had come to Cornerstone to die. He chose the time and the place, and Main Street became a battlefield.

SUNDANCE: OVERKILL
John Benteen

When a wealthy banker's daughter was kidnapped by the Cheyenne, he offered Sundance $10,000 to rescue the girl.

RIDE A LONE TRAIL
Gordon D. Shirreffs

The valley was about to explode into open range war. All it needed was the fuse and Ken Macklin was it.

HARD MAN WITH A GUN
Charles N. Heckelmann

After Bob Keegan lost the girl he loved and the ranch he had sweated blood to build, he had nothing left but his guts and his guns but he figured that was enough.

SUNDANCE: IRON MEN
Peter McCurtin

Sundance, assigned to save the railroad from a murder spree, soon came to realise that he'd have to fight fire with fire, bullets with bullets and death with death!